THE LIVING CAMPAIGN

A GUIDE FOR CREATING & MAINTAINING TABLETOP RPG CAMPAIGNS

Copyright © 2023 by John N McGowan

All rights reserved. This book or any portion thereof may not be reproduced or used in any manner whatsoever without the express written permission of the publisher except for the use of brief quotations in a book review. The mention of any company, person, or product is for informational purposes and not a challenge to the trademark concerned.

First Printing, 2023

ISBN 979-8-9896676-0-4

www.https://twitter.com/McGowanJohnN

Cover Art by Christopher Cant

TABLE OF CONTENTS

INTRODUCTION TO THE CONCEPT OF THE LIVING CAMPAIGN — 1

THE EXPECTATIONS UPON THE GAME MASTER — 5

THE EXPECTATIONS UPON THE PLAYER — 8

DEFINING THE RELATIONSHIP BETWEEN GAME MASTER & PLAYER — 10

PART I

IN PREPARATION FOR THE CAMPAIGN — 13

THE MECHANICAL FOUNDATION — 17

THE CREATION OF THE WORLD — 18

THE FIRST QUEST — 25

POPULATING THE WORLD: THE NON-PLAYER CHARACTER — 27

ADVENTURES BOTH GRAND AND SMALL & THE LIVING DUNGEON — 31

THE PASSAGE OF TIME & EXPLORING THE DUNGEON — 41

ALTERNATIVE PLAY: THEATER OF THE MIND — 47

UTILIZATION OF CHARACTER SKILLS — 50

ENCUMBRANCE & LOOT — 52

EXPERIENCE AWARDS & LEVEL GROWTH — 55

THE CAMPAIGN GROWS — 61

APPROACHING MASS COMBAT — 64

EXAMPLE DUNGEON: GROTTO OF THE WINTER CIRCLE — 68

PART II

DEFENDING THE METHOD	72
THE CASE FOR A MECHANICAL FOUNDATION	75
CREATE ONLY WHAT IS NECESSARY: NON-PLAYER CHARACTERS	77
HOW TO CREATE A WORLD	79
WHY TO CREATE A WORLD	84
APPLIED CHAOS IS A POWERFUL TOOL	85
NON-NEGOTIABLE: DEFINING THE PASSAGE OF TIME	89
CODIFYING THE DUNGEON CRAWL	98
FOR EVERY PLAYER, A MULTITUDE: MANY CHARACTERS PER PLAYER	102
THE SKILL LIST AS A "NON-GAME"	106
THE DUNGEON AS A LIVING ENTITY	110
ORGANICALLY GROWN ADVENTURES	115
TO THE VICTOR, THE SPOILS: HANDLING LOOT & ENCUMBRANCE	120
THROUGH EXPERIENCE, STUDY, & GREAT EFFORT: LEVELING UP	124
CAMPAIGNS GROW LIKE A MUSCLE	130
NON-NEGOTIABLE: THE PLAYER STRONGHOLD	135
NON-NEGOTIABLE: MASSED WARFARE	138
THE PERPETUAL MOTION MACHINE	142
TO THE PROLIFERATION OF TABLES	145

INTRODUCTION TO THE CONCEPT OF THE LIVING CAMPAIGN

Accepting the responsibility of running a campaign is a commitment that should be taken seriously.
The suggested seriousness with which the task should be approached, however, does not assume that the Game Master (GM) is destined to resent their participation as the Campaign Referee or be prevented from enjoying themselves as much as their players: while straining your imagination and creativity is a given, playing the game should still be positively anticipated as the prospective Game Master steadily becomes an expert in their craft.
To be good at anything requires some work to make it happen!

The Living Campaign was written to compile a set of standards and practices that will make long-term, highly enjoyable campaigns a replicable occurrence regardless of the preferred rules system of the Game Master. At present, significantly more players exist relative to the Game Masters who conduct the games they play in - an unfortunate amount of those campaigns either fail to launch or sputter to a halt as time goes on, further exacerbating the problem. That this outcome is so prevalent in the hobby community speaks to a deficiency in the quality of the resources available and commonly accepted advice for how to conduct a game.

There are simply not enough tables for everyone who would like to play. The obvious solution then...is to facilitate more tables!
While it is true that the various rulesets often have a chapter on, or even a book dedicated to, the creation and running of a campaign - it is also true that the majority of these works only go so far as to describe their view of what the Game Master's responsibility is,

followed by a series of bullet points that do not concretely lay out a method that is easily repeatable across many tables.

Much of this work is inspired by Gary Gygax's Dungeon Masters Guide and Players Handbook: works that speak authoritatively on **what ought to be done** with regard to the conducting of a campaign and are otherwise incredible resources for drawing inspiration - the best practices established in those books usually carry over into related descendant systems with only minor massaging. The original rulesets developed by influential figures like Gygax and Dave Arneson assumed a long-term, dynamic Campaign World where player agency was a given. This perception was the evolution of the incredible wargames campaigns conducted by Donald Featherstone and Tony Bath in the 1950s into the 1960s, where players were involved as leaders of nations in worlds created by Mr. Bath. They sent letters discussing intrigues, treaties, and even political marriages between family members (in the game of course)!

Which means: the methodology of *the Living Campaign* is not a new concept designed by myself, but an exploration of the injunctions and assumptions of a previous era with the intention of deriving a standardized set of best practices that can be applied to many present-day rulesets to help struggling Game Masters perhaps find an alternative method that more effectively draws out their talents and improves the work-to-play ratio so that they will escape the notorious specter of "GM Burnout".
Effective campaign design will cover for a great number of personal deficiencies in creativity and improvisational skills;

if the Game Master aspirant has the discipline to maintain accurate records of the various Campaign events and orders, then they are equipped to create a freeform sandbox that their players can affect and influence for many years to come.

In the pages ahead, there will be no qualifying statements of "this is just an opinion". I hold a sincere belief in the utility of the advice within this book - this is not to say that those who disregard the following instructions are bad people, but that this method of play is perhaps not for them.
Among the acquaintances, friends, and fellows in the hobby: a significant portion of them reject these injunctions out of hand, this Author would challenge any whose immediate reaction is terse dismissal to reconsider and attempt to sincerely follow the suggestions contained herein before they loudly condemn. If the reader can honestly say that they or their players were unsatisfied with the results, then I will have no choice but to respect my fellow GM's decision to refrain from permanent implementation.

If the reader is already running an ongoing campaign and wishes to attempt the use of this method, then they should open an honest dialogue with their players before attempting to conduct the Campaign in this manner; if the players would agree to try then the prospective GM should encourage them to exhibit a spirit of patience as new and unfamiliar territory is charted. A gaming group with a proper, healthy dynamic will make real attempts at compliance if their GM asks it of them, especially if the request is made with the intention of elevating the game and creating more fun and enjoyment at the table.

If the reader finds themselves the Game Master of campaign in decline, then what do they have to lose by attempting something different? Perhaps *the Living Campaign* will take root in a way that their previous attempts at longevity failed to do!

Ultimately, this book is for those who have found that the advice that they have received thus far in their Tabletop RPG careers have yet to produce a game that survives for a significant period of time - or that they seem to constantly burn out after a few months into the running of their campaigns.

THE EXPECTATIONS UPON THE GAME MASTER

The Game Master is expected to achieve rules fluency and be able to quickly arbitrate edge cases with regard to the rules in such a way that is satisfactorily fair to the players. It is certainly both unfair and unrealistic to expect immediate proficiency in this matter - it is important for the GM to maintain their drive to move forward and strive always to improve with each session played. This is true not just for the new GM but also for longtime veterans of the craft - it is not unheard of for a previously successful Game Master to eventually become content to rest on their laurels and allow their hard-earned talents to deteriorate from an overabundance of comfort and a lack of introspection.

The GM must cultivate within themselves the discipline to maintain the integrity of the game so that it maintains its vitality from week to week. As the Campaign grows in complexity and a multitude of characters are established within the setting, it is important that the GM continue to refine their process to keep their workload reasonable so as not to burn out.
The Game Master who succeeds in creating within themselves this discipline will not suffer in their craft and will eventually reach a state where the Campaign's growth will only minimally require consistency in the form of a few hours of concentrated work a week...usually by responding to player inquiries, populating a new locale with a few interesting personalities, or stocking their folder with a few more dungeons when they start to run low.

It is the responsibility of the GM to do their best in preserving the harmony of the table; this could mean impartially mediating disputes between two or more players, speaking to individuals that behave in an unsportsmanlike manner, and/or consigning to exile those players who refuse to be rehabilitated and persist in antisocial behavior. If a ruling is made, then the GM should abide confidently in their decision unless some truly egregious error in judgment is pointed out. It is not prudent to bend every time the players raise objections to the Game Master's arbitration and it is more than appropriate to allocate space for such objections at the end of the session or privately through phone or text message.

At the end of the day, the Game Master MUST maintain control of their table and the Campaign not for their own sake, but for the sake of the other players in the Campaign. Too often, it is advised that the GM acquiesce always to demands of the players and indulge their whims in some misguided attempt at accommodation...of course, framing a significant portion of "GM Advice" this way is uncharitable - though the results of common platitudes like "talk to your players" indicate that listeners too-often interpret that to mean "never put your foot down if people get mad".

In these cases, a firm line must be drawn between reasonable accommodation and appeasement of a belligerent! Perhaps the "Rule of Cool" has its place, but its invocation is no excuse for the GM to allow themselves to be bullied into submission when they well and truly disagree with the viability of the players' undertaking!

Now while the above is true, the GM should take care to discern their heart and be suspicious of the animus that lives there. The benevolence of firm, fair, and friendly arbitration is nothing at all like the pathological overreaction against any who dare question or voice a dissenting opinion. Resorting to authoritarian command of a situation is a tool with limited utility once it has been subject to overuse; there can BE no game at all if *all* the players decide to leave or are otherwise banished from the table! The GM who assumes fully the authority of their station AND the responsibility that goes with that authority will be able to encourage the flourishing of new friendships and the deepening of friendly bonds. The GM who understands their responsibility is in a position to abolish the petty bickering that can so easily arise in a cooperative game of this type.

To act in order to preserve the harmony of their friends and the Campaign is no tyranny and, in fact, much good can be done by the campaign referee who understands their place in the schema of the overall game!

THE EXPECTATIONS UPON THE PLAYER

Much has been made of the Game Master's responsibility to the Campaign both in this work and the broader conversation around the hobby. Comparatively less discussed is the responsibility of each player around the table and what ought to be expected of them during their time as members of the Campaign. Many distressing stories exist of derangements and insanities that have manifested around tables, but the conversation around these are entirely disconnected from the large body of instruction and lessons of etiquette that take place within the hobby. The vast majority of the lessons, essays, videos, and podcasts on the subject of GM/Player Relations are almost entirely aimed at the Game Masters, while precious few discuss what is expected of the players themselves.

The players have not only obligations to one another, but obligations to the GM. The Game Master of the Campaign MUST be accepted as the omega within the realm of rules arbitration for the game by the players. It is impolite and crass for the player to object against rulings that impact them negatively but enthusiastically accept anything positive that comes to them; any sort of dispute that is truly unbearable to the player perhaps warrants a bit of introspection about whether they would like to continue with the Campaign. A GM who exhibits a pathological need for control and commits an endless number of coercions against the players around the table may not even warrant a conversation - it is perhaps better to just excuse oneself from the game.

The ultimate recourse the player has against the unlimited authority of the GM is the unspoken, implied threat of simply abandoning the Campaign.

To argue about such and such ruling every time is to dilute the power of the implicit threat and make expulsion that much more attractive - under such circumstances, it is possible to be booted from the game to the applause of the other players!

A player is expected to maintain sportsmanlike conduct at all times. While everyone falls short of this from time to time, it is no excuse for players to consistently allow themselves to act belligerently with their fellows and/or the GM. When they encounter a setback or frustration within the game, the superior player will accept the outcome and work to turn the tables back in their favor or find a way to otherwise mitigate their losses. A player should always seek to elevate their ability and comprehension of the Campaign; at no point should an individual decide that they have learned everything that matters and cease their attempts at ever increasing proficiency both from a mechanical standpoint and a characterological one.

After all, the Tabletop RPG is a cooperative adventure game that requires social skills as much as it does a tolerance for arithmetic and memorization. If others routinely lose interest in playing with an individual across different social settings, perhaps that individual should turn their gaze inward and cultivate the virtues that will see them invited back week after week.

DEFINING THE RELATIONSHIP BETWEEN GAME MASTER & PLAYER

The Living Campaign assumes a proper relationship between the players and their GM. A player should trust the Game Master to rule firmly and fairly, this INCLUDES rulings against the player's desires; they are expected to be honest in their dealings and good sportsmen.

In return for this loyalty and trust, the GM MUST hold up their end of the bargain. They must not unduly inflict character death, or revel in the players' failure, or attempt to hijack the table in the name of a favorite NPC who may as well be the hero of a novel. A common emotional trap a GM can fall into is resenting the players for not approaching the details of their setting with the same reverence the GM has. They will joke, they will make assumptions apropos of nothing, they will not care about grand histories, nor be intimidated by villains. They are not actors, there is no script: they may crack a joke at an NPC funeral - accept this before ever organizing a game.

That said, a table ought to be curated in such a way that the various participants all agree to engage in the game with one another in good faith. The GM must try to anticipate potential personality conflicts when forming a gaming group and be ready to step in when tempers flare. BENEVOLENT authority must remain resolutely in the hands of the Game Master for the sake of all their friends around the table. BENEVOLENT authority can only be maintained if the players willingly cede them such power - the reciprocal nature of the game is a delicate balance...or otherwise devolves into tyrannical behavior or baying of a mob.

This harmony is best achieved if the aspiring GM simply employs some discernment when sending the invites.

An assembled group of honest sportsmen provides a GM with the most powerful tool that they can possibly get: players that will be able to fill functions on the behalf of the GM and in service to their fellows - these are the jobs like Party Caller, Quartermaster, Mapper, Diarist, Banker. Delegation of bookkeeping tasks from the GM to a party of players that are trusted to be honest will instill in the players a sense of ownership over the activities within the game. The Quartermaster will have no choice but to pay attention when loot is obtained...since the rest of the group will look to them when they get treasure and items. Who will have the time to be checking their social media in such an environment?
What's more: they will begin to enjoy the work they do, they are pulling their weight within the party and perform an important function.

If the prospective GM is able to cultivate such an environment at their table, they will be fully ready to implement the guidelines for etiquette established previously, as their players will trust them to be in their right mind and fully intent on creating the most fun experience that they can possibly manage.

PART I

IN PREPARATION FOR THE CAMPAIGN

The methodology of *The Living Campaign* is only complicated insofar as it is not broadly known and does not have large bodies of work and resources buttressing it for new players and Game Masters. In describing the method, the prospective GM may balk at what they perceive as requiring an enormous preparatory effort that assumes a working knowledge of many computer applications and a talent for organization.

The nature of the prep work from which the actual game will be derived is discussed in the following chapters. This chapter is concerned only with the physical needs associated with the actual logistics of running a Campaign in this manner.

A campaign journal of some kind will be required, preferably one that can be stored comfortably tucked behind the GM screen (or similar barrier) but that the GM still retains access to for quick note taking. Any notebook will do - logging the date and player activity is easy enough. Writing it out in the journal this way charts a natural progression that is a chronologically organized reference for the GM to track concurrent activities of players and their characters. Once so written, it is easy to make the necessary rolls on the myriad outcomes of out-of-session results to player decisions; this is not merely for keeping track of players however - keeping a journal helps the GM remember to roll for the outputs of generated events, faction movements, and the migratory patterns of hostile creatures - as examples.

Several d20 systems are supported through apps for phones and mobile devices and there are endless resources for tracking encounters, turns, and creatures of all kinds. This is one area of the game where the common wisdom is often relevant and helpful; thousands of hours of text and videos exist to help the new GM get an idea of what it is to run encounters for the game in a concrete, mechanically accurate way (how do the bonuses work? How are player turns arbitrated? Etc.). Though it should be noted that the design architecture of encounters are not comparable between *the Living Campaign* and the common, contemporary game; only the rules applications for things like turn order or character statistics will remain more or less the same. If apps are either not wanted or unavailable for the chosen ruleset, it is recommended then that GMs keep scrap paper with which to record the hit points of hostiles and record damage for NPCs and monsters that may end up in combat with the player characters.

It is usually enough to have a general idea of what the regional monsters and NPCs are capable of, rather than become intimate with every detail and possibility for their use. Looking through a magic-user's spell list and picking a handful of the most likely candidates for casting is unlikely to be noticed by the players. Taking the time to familiarize oneself with the layout of the various rulebooks and having practiced methods of information retrieval on-hand will dramatically reduce the time required to figure out the use of monsters or NPCs involved in an unexpected encounter. The unexpected happens and there is no shame in taking a few minutes to get it ready. Knowing HOW to look it up quickly makes this process much less painful when it occurs during play.

While there are enormous bodies of proprietary combat encounters and dungeon maps with elaborate dungeons, town centers, and other set pieces, they are largely only relevant in very specific circumstances and scenarios. Hiding the areas that the players can't see with pre-made map tiles is a clumsy affair that rarely succeeds in the task...

Vinyl battle mats are some of the most common GM tools used at the table as they can be adapted to depict any sort of circumstance or environment. The primary advantage of mats of this type is they give the GM the ability to draw out a scenario as the various parts of it become visible to the players. It is fairly simple and quick to transcribe a dungeon map drawn on normal graph paper to the mat used at the table. The pre-drawn battlemats might be higher in quality, but for the purposes of presenting a truly open-ended game, their utility is limited.

Tokens for the players ought to be distinct enough so that they will not be confused about who is who; tokens for monsters ought to fill the same criteria. I used 1 inch by 1 inch washers with pictures of monsters glued to them in the beginning of my GMing career - a very inexpensive solution; my table has since grown to include a great many miniatures and pawns that are much higher quality - which are an enjoyed visual on the table...but their actual, practical utility over the washers is minimal.

Alternatively, it is entirely possible to run dungeons of all kinds through the use of standard graph paper and "Theater of the Mind" (refer to ALTERNATIVE PLAY: THEATER OF THE MIND on pg. 47), where miniatures are used to depict marching order and distances are broadly determined through the graph paper map and narration by the GM and the players.

This method is inexpensive and easy to set up in almost no time at all. It suits more imaginative players since they have no issue constructing the imagery of unfolding events entirely within their mind's eye.

Lastly, the prospective GM will need players. While an open door policy is admirable, it would behoove the GM to have some method of vetting potential players at their table. This is not to say "never allow newcomers", but is more of a call for GMs to take responsibility for creating cohesion among the group members; devising some criteria by which invites are issued will help prevent predatory, pathological, or otherwise incompatible players from inflicting themselves upon others at the table. Many, many horror stories that exist out in the greater community could have been prevented by a GM who took their portion of the responsibility toward the maintenance of their table's culture seriously. While this won't solve every potential pitfall associated with running the game, and no filter is perfect, HAVING a filter is vastly preferable to NOT having a filter!

And that's it.

The required materials more-or-less do not extend beyond the above described items. The Campaign is reasonably able to be managed with an inexpensive list of visual aids, best practices, a campaign journal, and (of course) dice. The methodology of *the Living Campaign* is deceptively simple: the meticulous plotting of world events is not necessary, but that is not to say that laziness is permitted here; diligent recording of information and proper use of Gamemastery tools to interpret that information is still certainly a task requiring the discipline of the GM that tries it.

THE MECHANICAL FOUNDATION

A foundational ruleset is an obvious requirement for beginning a campaign. This will likely be the easiest part of the entire endeavor, as the players and GM will probably have some rulebook in mind before they ever get together to play...however the choice will color the experience permanently. The specific values of treasure, the creation/development of Non-Player Characters (NPCs), and what is considered appropriate awarding of equipment and experience is information that will be inferred from the foundational ruleset. For example, if your rules assume a silver-based economy, then the overall value of character endeavors will be determined in terms of silver pieces in the format established within the book the aspirant has chosen. Many systems of varied types can be adapted for use in this style of play and is not exactly wholly reliant on the d20 dice roll...in fact, any game where the core gameplay loop involves the procurement of treasure and the conquering of adversity will fit nicely into the rules standard laid out here.

The rules addenda and guidelines established here will prepare the reader and the reader's table to play with the Foundational Ruleset by organically allowing them to create multiple characters both as a product of their individual stories and due to "reasonable" Player Character (PC) death. Following this guide will mechanically encourage the players to become well read in the chosen ruleset, only the disinterested will fail in this task and naturally wash out of the campaign with (hopefully) no hard feelings. If all goes well, your players will become experts in multiple aspects of your game and be able to come together in order to help both you and their fellows as the Campaign continues to evolve.

THE CREATION OF THE WORLD

Creating a campaign setting is broadly understood to be a daunting task. I disagree with this assessment. The creation of the setting is daunting for writers of novels and screenplays, but this guide is not interested in such things - our craft is a feat of engineering and implementation of a design philosophy. We are engaging in a dice game, so how appropriate then is it to generate a world through the intentional application of chaos? Through smart use of random tables and a little bit of creative ingenuity we will create a campaign setting that is equipped to evolve organically over a period of years and decades and we will do it over mere days or weeks (depending on your free time!) not months or years.

A few things must be determined by the Game Master entirely on their own: what is the genre of the campaign setting? Fantasy? Science Fiction? Space Opera? Steampunk? Post-Apocalyptic?
The genre will help inform the GM as to which real-world nations and traditions to draw upon for their campaign. I am of the opinion that basing the campaign's cultures on the cultures and factions of the real-world saves time, energy, and more easily fosters player investment as they recognize titles and forms. There will still be much room for creativity and a unique world without an entire separate dossier on a completely alien syntax and governmental type. There is no shame in borrowing from the vast well of history to give one's Campaign a certain "realistic" quality that allows players to better slip into a willing suspension of disbelief.

When the genre is decided, it is time to generate the landmass that the players will be interacting with. There are near-infinite resources to determine things like the shape of the land, the type of biomes within a country, etc.

The prospective GM could easily find map images on their search engine of choice and trace over conglomerations to generate continents of all kinds of shapes with authentic coastlines. Similarly there are many methods for generating biomes, though I usually prefer to consult real world maps and use those as a guideline for how many mountains, hills, plains, forests, rivers, etc. exist in a single contiguous landmass. Frankly, your players are not likely to notice if biomes are not 100% "realistic". Any noticed inconsistency can be handwaved post hoc (magic accident, technology run amok, etc.).

Incidentally, a full world map is entirely unnecessary - a playable area consisting of a single page of hex paper can be generated as needed, with more hexes added as players travel. Eventually, a world map will begin to form!

The next step in the process involves generating natural resources. This will help you visualize the economic conditions of your unborn nation(s). Knowing that a certain section of the map produces large amounts of iron, for example, informs the GM that perhaps this area of the world is known for its incredible metallurgy or the existence of a cluster of gold ore mines indicates the wealth of the lords of a region, incredible public works and art could be generated from the cities built here.

Most importantly, resource rich areas that exist at the edge of borders is an impetus for conflict between lords and nations. Players beginning in these areas might note the tension in a town as they brace for unforeseen foreign raiders who plunder their gold stores. Many stories can be generated simply by the placement of valuable, shiny rocks!

There are three primary land types that I consider while creating any campaign map hex:

1) Lowlands
2) Hills
3) Mountains

A more geologically minded GM may find that they'd prefer an array of types, as that is their interest, but it would be uncommon for players to notice anything amiss if something specific was missing...and it is a better use of a Game Master's limited time to keep it relatively simple to better facilitate planning their Campaign for their table.

Lowlands would be most likely to have tracts of arable land for the growing of crops and the pasturing of animals. The breadbasket of nations will be located in these areas. Swamps might fall here, alternatively.

Hills could be considered a middle ground between Lowland and Mountain - they could conceivably contain valuable ores as well as arable grassland; the foothills of a mountain range, for example.

Mountains will not have much in the way of land for animals, wheat, or cotton but are a likely source of ores used in luxury and construction; a mining town would be built in a mountain range.

A way to determine the likelihood for a hex to contain farms, mines, and quarries will be necessary. I have assigned the percentage chance of certain features of industry like so at my table:

1) Lowlands
   a) 10% chance of a quarry (max: 1)
   b) 10% chance of a mine
   c) 90% chance of farmable land
2) Hills
   a) 40% chance of a quarry (max: 1)
   b) 40% chance of a mine
   c) 40% chance of farmable land
3) Mountains
   a) 80% chance of a quarry (max: 1)
   b) 80% chance of a mine
   c) 0% chance of farmable land

Rolling a percentage die at or below the percent chance of a mine, for example, in the territory type means that 1 mine is located there. Roll percentage again, reducing the chance by 10%, and if the die rolls are at or below the new success chance there is another mine. Upon rolling higher than the current percentage, there will be no more active mines in the hex.

Ex: Mountains have an 80% chance of a mine, the GM rolls their percentage die and gets a 58% - there is 1 mine. The chance is reduced to 70% and the GM rolls again, they get a 45% this time - there are 2 mines. The chance is further reduced to 60% and the GM rolls percentage again, though this time they roll a 62%, which is a failure. This territory will only have 2 mines in operation.

At which point, determining the ore type of the mine is a matter of writing down the possible ores that could potentially populate the geography of the map and assigning them a number range.

I use the following probability to determine the ore found in the node:

Mine Type (1d12):
> 1-4: iron
> 5: adamantite
> 6: mithral
> 7-8: copper
> 9-10: cold iron
> 11: silver
> 12: gold

A d12 is rolled and the result is assigned to a mine in the region. The value of the ores will likely be included in whichever ruleset the aspiring GM chooses as their foundation. The reader can add or remove ore types as they need or adjust the type of dice rolled.

For farmland, roll the percentage die similarly to the above criteria though with one difference: every success adds +1d20 to the roll to determine the number of miles of farmland or pastures.

Ex: Lowlands have a 90% chance to have farmland; the GM rolls percentage and gets 82%, they note that they have 1d20 to roll. The chance is reduced to 80% and the GM rolls percentage again, they get 67% - another 1d20 is added. Chance is reduced to 70%, this time the GM rolls a 78%. A failure. They have 2d20 in their pool and roll it: the first d20 rolls a 19 and the other rolls a 12; this territory will have 31 miles of farmland in it.

The aspiring GM can play with the percentages as they like or even add little tweaks of their own. I prefer to include a rule that allows a hex with a river to reroll 1 failed farmland percentage chance roll to simulate better soil fertility from the river's presence.

To determine the value of the land's bounty, it must be remembered that the exact value in coins of the land's resources will likely be informed by the foundational system you have chosen for your campaign. What decides the final tally in this area is determining the economic standard by which all other values are judged. In the eyes of this GM: the standard is the Dungeon!
It is the treasures contained therein that spur the party forward, that allow them to expand their popular reach and outfit them with incredible equipment. No natural resource should be so valuable that they overshadow the Dungeon too early in a Player Character's career and prematurely remove their need for adventure...but then natural resources ought not to be so valueLESS that the players do not feel the pull to stake their claims upon the land that they adventure in!

Assuming the mine types above - it should be determined by the GM just how many dungeons the various resources and commodities are worth, with dangers and jealous Others trying to wrest control of the more valuable ones. For example, perhaps a gold mine is worth 2 dungeons worth of gold pieces per month, whereas an iron mine is worth 0.2 dungeons of gold pieces per month? Surely, the gold mine will attract the attention of people and groups who would prefer to acquire their wealth without having to extract it from the evil places beneath the earth.

With the actual physical makeup of the land completed, the GM will determine the political boundaries of the societies that populate it. One could borrow from a method in reality: determining borders according to geographic markers like mountains, rivers, and forests; perhaps a country lost a war in the past and so lost control of a section of their former borders to a rival nation. Incongruities can beg questions from the observer and rationalizing the existence of said incongruities is good low-stakes improvisational practice for the GM.

Now while the generation of an entire planet's worth of continental landmass is doable, it is not strictly necessary to have the entire thing mapped/established before the first session; this can be done over the course of the game with areas of the map filled in as necessary. It ought to be enough to create a hub where the player characters can rest, sell equipment, and otherwise deposit loot; a dungeon or two will be enough to keep the players locally rooted. Upon acquiring said loot, the player characters will likely begin pursuing their backstories and other motivations, which can be organically added to the campaign as needed.

With the generation of a landmass, infused with resources like gold, iron, farmland, etc, and populated with characters of varying personalities - the GM has prepared the area that the players are setting forth upon. There will be the temptation at this stage to endlessly tweak and alter the particulars of the world - you must resist this urge...above all other things it is most important to GET TO PLAYING. The prospective GM cannot learn until they actually begin to play their game.

What should the first adventure of a campaign look like? There is a tried and true method...

THE FIRST QUEST

For many, there is considerable heartache over creating the perfect hook to start the perfect adventure. Advice ranges from "just start in a tavern and don't worry about it!" to "NEVER start in a tavern because it's boring!" - all this time and energy is wasted on one of the most simple aspects of the Campaign creation process: getting players to go on an adventure.

Before even agreeing to join the game, the players should be instructed to create characters whose goals can only be solved by the slaying of monsters and the acquisition of loot. Nothing about the game can accommodate the individual who only wants to remain a merchant of knick-knacks or a blacksmith's apprentice. Establishing this early removes the need for some adequately compelling adventure hook since a town can have a basic monster problem, put the call out for help, and when people arrive they can point to the issue and say "there's gold over there, please kill all the monsters". Complexity can (and WILL) come later as the player characters begin to adventure and find the time and resources to begin looking into their more complex issues.

For now, a simplistic situation that is easily understood will provide the players much needed direction as they contend with the dramatic increase in the freedom allotted to them in the format of *the Living Campaign*. Only the first session of a brand new campaign with brand new players would need to have a quest like this in order to provide participants with that initial grounding in an unfamiliar world. Even players experienced in the mechanics of the foundational ruleset would do well to have their initial foray into the Campaign done from the beginning of a Player Character's career.

While the numbers and statistics will be familiar, their application will be alien - the heretofore successful strategies of play may be found to no longer be viable when the complexity of the world begins to weigh on their builds (if the chosen ruleset has such a thing as "builds"). It is a disservice to them to begin playing a PC at a higher level - they may have chosen abilities or skills that will hurt their overall enjoyment of the game, since they are likely more used to a curated experience that caters to their character's strengths. As much as they might protest, it would be better to insist that they begin at the lowest level and work up from there. After a single session in my Campaign, long-time players of certain rulesets begrudgingly admitted that perhaps beginning at level 1 was the right idea as the methods they had employed as a matter of course failed to produce the results they were used to.

Upon completing this first quest and looting what they can grab from the dungeon, they will be equipped, leveled, and have the pocket money required to begin the pursuit of things throughout the world where they will meet many interesting and unique characters.

But who are the people that live within the Campaign?

POPULATING THE WORLD: THE NON-PLAYER CHARACTER

Non-Player Characters (NPCs) are the personalities that populate the milieu and provide the cast of allies and villains for the player characters to negotiate with and test their mettle against. Whether the aspiring GM would prefer to hand craft each character, apply some method of random generation, or a mixture of the two is largely a matter of personal taste and interest in such things.

It is far more likely, regardless of actual work input, that players will project personalities and perceptions onto the many NPCs that they meet; it is a triviality to indulge their initial impressions or subvert them - as their reactions will serve as the springboard that informs the GM's performance. A bullet-pointed list of general tendencies is usually plenty for determining the NPC's initial behavior within the Campaign. Reaction rolls are useful for creating varied NPCs that behave uniquely and stand out in the players' minds. Reaction rolls are a percentage chance that determines the NPC's initial reaction upon meeting a Player Character or Characters. These rolls are modified by the PCs' Charisma (or equivalent social statistic) and affect that NPC's demeanor when the players first interact with them: sometimes NPCs will like the Player Characters, sometimes they might find them suspicious...just like in life, people are unpredictable.

The concept of the **Reaction Roll** is further explored with regard to monsters in the next chapter (refer to ADVENTURES BOTH GRAND AND SMALL & THE LIVING DUNGEON; see pg.31).

There is a temptation that beckons for all GMs to overdesign their NPCs, pouring hours and hours into a character's motivations and backstory only for the players to be entirely disinterested in the NPC and attempt to leave them behind at first opportunity. There are many cases where exasperated GM's recount how their players sent a crucial would-be ally on their way only to become enamored with the random tavern patron they were pumping for information! Such occurrences are why it is best to have only a handful of outward facing characteristics planned for each potential personality. There is plenty of time to negotiate the deeper motivations of those characters who actually graduate to "recurring".

It is my recommendation that the following personae be determined before the first session begins:
1) The head of state for the country
2) The leader of the starting area community
3) The owners of the local places of business
4) The local spiritual leader(s)
5) At least 1 villain that will serve as the first antagonist of the Campaign

A handful of random personalities will suffice. These need not be anything other than personality traits - generic physical characteristics can simply be improvised (short/long brown hair and brown eyes is valid!); overconcern with being descriptively derivative is not productive or useful in the overall schema of the Campaign's construction. Frankly, the players are unlikely to notice.

Be aware that as the game continues and the scope begins to expand, the players will likely require the services of all types of hirelings for things like the carrying of items, building of strongholds, the forming of military bands, etc.

There will come a time when at least one of the PCs will want to project their influence over longer distances as they find that they can't be everywhere at once or are otherwise occupied with other activities; for example, a mercenary force can harass the occupants of a dungeon that the PCs were unable to complete due to some unforeseen circumstance, preventing the Dungeon's inhabitants from fully replenishing their ranks or healing from their wounds.

Consider taking the time to create standard templates for basic/common non-player characters: average ability score spreads that can be applied based on the job or other criteria of the NPC in question. Every basic soldier of a specific type can have the same chance of a successful strike and nearly the same amount of hit points and other defenses relative to each other. A town militia spearman can safely be assumed to be similarly trained everywhere they appear. This idea extends even to the basic laborers and citizens of the milieu that they need not be overly detailed - assuming a small number of hit points and an overall lack of combat ability or armor defense is plenty of information to statistically determine what a serf is capable of, for example. No need to build out full character sheets for characters of such humble origins, they are unlikely to be skilled in much other than their profession and otherwise not able to withstand trained adventurers if the situation calls for the involvement of their persons.

The players will be unaware that only the most relevant statistics of the NPC has been chosen; in the unlikely event that specific scores for rolls are required from a recurring NPC commoner, then it is possible that such a character has earned a full character sheet, but these things are best left up to the GM's discretion and personal taste.

ADVENTURES BOTH GRAND AND SMALL & THE LIVING DUNGEON

Planning for a Living Campaign is different from the common methods and advice offered by many. With the method described herein, your world will generate heroes and villains the longer you play within it, but their place in those categories will likely be determined by the specific PCs.

The PCs are still expected to have histories and backgrounds - they came from somewhere, they have loves and hates, they have hopes and dreams. Your players will generate their character's motivations and then it is your job to incorporate those motivations into the Machinery of the World. Player Characters will be relatively powerless in the beginning, as it is my recommendation that even experienced players begin at the lowest level. The players will need resources, money, equipment, and clout in order to accomplish their goals.

All of these things can be acquired by finding interesting things out in the world, killing what guards it, and bringing the treasures back for personal gain. The devising of a simple method for generation of dungeons within a hex will benefit the GM greatly in this task;

I use the following method to determine the size, strength, and contents of the Dungeon:

> Roll 1d20 for each 6 mile by 6 mile square located within a hex: on a roll of "1" there will be a dungeon located there.
> In isolated wilderness: roll 1d20 to determine the level of the monsters within.
> In rural civilization: roll 1d12 to determine the level of monsters
> In settled areas: roll 1d6 to determine the level of monsters.
> Roll 1d20 to decide how many floors within the dungeon complex
> Roll 2d8 for each floor to determine the number of rooms located there
>
> ---
>
> Roll 1d20 for each room on the floor, record the result:
>
> ---
>
> 1-12 : empty
> 13-14: monster only
> 15-17: monster and treasure
> 18: special (a room with some unique function)
> 19: trick/trap
> 20: treasure

Of course, it is perfectly reasonable to simply set the number of floors or the level of the monsters within a dungeon by fiat, if its circumstances would be better served; if the GM wants to build a twenty floor megadungeon, then they will not be barred from it!

In the past, I have used a handy generator called **"One Page Dungeon" by watabou** which quickly generates dungeon maps based on a number of tags that determine the overall makeup of a dungeon instantly; though currently I prefer to draw out the basic structure of the Dungeon on graph paper. It is easy enough to populate rooms with monsters, traps, and treasure relatively quickly with the map already made.

These dungeons do not need to be overly elaborate or exhaustive, since they are just a vehicle by which the players can gain sums of treasure, fight monsters, and hone their teamwork. While the above method for random generation is useful, perhaps the Campaign requires a specific dungeon type or the GM simply feels like making something for their campaign world...then by all means they should go ahead and make it! It is important to note that a dungeon need not always be an underground danger-pit. The Dungeon is a *concept* - a city block can be a dungeon, a section of forest can be a dungeon, a large enough boat, even, can be a dungeon!

Random Treasure Tables are great tools used to populate points of interest out in the wilds of the campaign world with money, items, and other treasures. It is best to use tables that are generous in the coinage they give and quickly allow players the means to get stronger, driving them forward enthusiastically. Sometimes these generators will produce *overly* generous piles of gold, it is recommended that such sums either be trapped or guarded (regardless of whether or not a monster was initially determined to be in this room); unattended gold piles are sure to maintain themselves through the determined predations of the things that guard them...whether that be from dangerous traps or the efforts of monsters, otherwise why hasn't anyone stolen them yet?

The GM ought to be considerate where they place treasure and the circumstances surrounding the placement of treasure; they should neither be overly generous or stingy or bloodthirsty. The *overall* goal should be that the risk will match the reward...hardly a novel concept.

The foundational ruleset will have the costs of all kinds of equipment types; surviving a dungeon should be a rewarding experience for the Player Character. A single dungeon is likely to provide enough money for new weapons and armor, a tidy chunk of experience points, with enough gold left over to grease palms and negotiate with associate NPCs should the player characters like to pursue their backgrounds with their legitimately acquired gains. Some Game Masters might choose to populate the world with a Dungeon already picked clean of loot - allowing for the occasional dud is certainly a viable method, but is also one that will cause many a player to (understandably) wail and gnash their teeth!

Whether or not a Dungeon always has treasure is the prerogative of the GM, but they should consider that a consistent lack of reward makes for unenthusiastic players if the condition persists for too long.

The final component of the Dungeon is the **Random Encounter Table**; the concept is often ignorantly derided as a dirty word in many gaming circles...however, proper utilization of the random encounter can inject tension in the form of the terrifying unknown into many adventures. A random encounter table ought to come in two parts:

1) The method by which the monster or NPC is chosen
2) The disposition of said monster or NPC

Perhaps the party finds themselves exploring a goblin burrow - the goblins are often hostile to intruders and the GM has rolled on their encounter table, indicating that a troupe has moved down the hall in the party's direction. A second roll for disposition is made and it seems the goblins have caught sight of a shiny bauble hooked to the belt of one of the PCs...they look to be willing to negotiate! The goblins might give map information or a description of their chief. Maybe the PCs ultimately decide they don't take chances and pick a fight anyway or they negotiate further after discovering that these goblins do not like their own chief and wouldn't mind a change in management.

The encounter is not always required to be a slog ending in violence! Played right, the GM will find themselves curious as to what their Grand Machine will hurl at the players!

An example of an encounter table is shown below:

Every 10 min (1 turn): roll 1d6; on a roll of "1" roll below
Floor 1: 1d6; 1: Monster Group 1a, Monster Group 1b 2: Monster Group 2 3: Monster Group 3 4: Monster Group 4a, Monster Group 4b, Monster Group 4c 5: Monster Group 5 6: Monster Group 6
Disposition: Base 50% + Charisma Bonus/Penalty + Outsider Penalty: -35% **Success by more than 20%**: friendly/willing to help **Success by less than 20%**: neutral/non-hostile **Failure by less than 10%**: hostile, not immediately aggressive **Failure by 10% or more**: hostile, immediately aggressive

A 1d6 roll determines the monster encountered and illustrates just how many monsters are wandering about; in the above example, two groups of monsters can potentially be encountered (one at a time), if those are dealt with then no more may be encountered for that number.

The disposition roll, also called "reaction roll", is modified by the total Charisma (or equivalent, depending on foundational ruleset) of the PCs and a percentage die is rolled to determine the overall disposition of the encountered creature. This is not applicable to mindless monsters of course (like skeletons, for example); these might always attack or otherwise listen to their orders, if applicable. This list can be populated with other intruders into the dungeon and as such, those intruders are not influenced by the Outsider Penalty. This means that encounters with rival explorers are less likely to descend into immediate violence since they are surrounded by a common foe, though it is not impossible for such things to occur, depending on both the roll and the overall likeability of the PCs.

Each successive floor can have different potential monster groups or maybe more fearsome versions of higher-floor creatures. Each dungeon should have encounter tables that represent the monsters roaming its halls, these creatures do not simply materialize out of the ether...they are assumed to be present, but they just haven't run into the player characters quite yet. The encounter is an abstraction of their movement, saving the GM from having to move 6 to 10 monster groups through the dungeon.

Any dungeon created in the manner described should have had its relative danger level determined at the beginning of its creation - with monsters and treasure being chosen to fit that scale. Following a rule of thumb so that there are dungeons available to parties of varying levels is recommended.

For example, for new parties I would prepare 3 to 4 low-level dungeons, a mid-level dungeon, and a high level dungeon for the starting hex. Those dungeons that are too strong will have several hints that this is the case so that the party might react accordingly and search for a mark that better matches their current ability. The too-powerful dungeons exist as a marker, signaling that the PCs should approach cautiously if they are unsure of what is inside a particular ruin or other somesuch structure. Players should be encouraged to have a back-up character, before the start of the first session, since the ever present threat of death looms most menacingly at the start of a PC's life as an adventurer.

The Game Master equipped with Random Treasure Tables, 3 to 5 pre-prepped dungeons, and Random Encounter and Disposition Tables can generate a consistent experience of tension, danger, and fun that encourages the players to seek out more dungeons - always hungry for the resources they need to further establish themselves within the world.

When players have looted large amounts of treasure, they will eventually tire of renting rooms from the inn and will instead begin to consider the purchase of property and/or the construction of permanent lodgings where they can store their loot and house their hirelings. Perhaps they will be granted lordships over a hex or open merchant shops where they will be able to generate income of their own!

If you are running in 1:1 time (refer to THE PASSAGE OF TIME & EXPLORING THE DUNGEON, pg. 41) then you will have the preparatory time needed to generate interesting quests and events based on these expansions by the players. Perhaps an employee has stolen a large sum of gold, or a rival lord begins to burn their farms and ransack the grainhouses? The players are not the only ones able to have an income and they will likely encounter more and more dangerous individuals as they rise up the socio-economic ladder.

Multiple problems will begin to arise for the PCs as they become stronger, in such cases they may not want to deal with lesser issues. Trusted hirelings and followers might be turned into PCs themselves, the players can enjoy playing a different class or taking care of lower stakes business while their favorite PCs are indisposed due to some long-term activity. Multiple characters generated in this way will each come with new origins and motivations. Each has the potential to add new villains to the world (as well as new potential allies); thus, the GM has freed themselves from the tyranny of the narrative railroad. What if your prospective players have given you no such grand personalities to be memorable villains? It does not matter...the treasure calling out from myriad dungeons will force the players to interact with the world. All you must do as the GM is talk to them ahead of time, while preparing the Campaign, and let them know that whatever they decide to play, they are adventurers and will need to make the ACTIVE PURSUIT of adventure a shared character trait!

Preparing a handful of NPC adventurers to be introduced via random encounter tables either out in the wilderness or down in the dungeon will help round out a cast of personalities and inject spontaneity - facilitating a "lived in" quality that players are almost always delighted by. These NPCs might be friendly or hostile, related to one or more of the PCs, or completely random. This is simply an advisory to have a few in your repertoire, they might come in handy if, say, a PC is searching the city for a lead on his missing sister, for example, and they can tap adventuring acquaintances for help in such matters.

For many players, the idea that their agency does not end with the conclusion of the session will probably require an adjustment period as they acclimate and the above scenarios may be slow to occur at first. Encouraging player action should be two-pronged: the first is to "pull" them along by helping them brainstorm ideas or remind them about their background events or personal interests they created with the character they built. It is no crime to offer ideas and encouragement to help them overcome "analysis paralysis": the overthinking that comes with a sudden overabundance of options. Providing their imagination with a carrot that entices them to choose a direction might be just what they require in order to get their creative energy flowing.

The second prong is the characters, factions, creatures, and events in the campaign setting itself that require some decision to be made. The crush of available options will be mitigated if some clear and present danger or circumstance requires the attention of the player character. An outside event will "push" players to move and help them overcome their initial trepidation by providing a point to fixate on and learn what they are able to do.

Together these are "push" and "pull" and are not required to be implemented in any particular order, but are a matter of the specific needs of specific players. Some players only need a few ideas seeded in order to fully immerse themselves to go forward while others may need to have that outside event to help narrow their options while they find their comfort zone.

Just as the running of a campaign in this way should be taken slowly, playing in it will follow the same logic.

Should the GM require a more concrete example of dungeon preparation: a short example dungeon has been provided at the end of Part I.

THE PASSAGE OF TIME & EXPLORING THE DUNGEON

It is of the utmost importance to the integrity of a campaign for the GM to establish some method for tracking the passage of time. A Living Campaign is not a narrative in the traditional sense: it *contains* narratives, but the world itself is not merely a stage for the telling of a single primary storyline, it is an organic thing that the players will attempt to impose their will upon and which will, in turn, resist this imposition. As such, you will need to have a method of determining the movement of factions, adventurers, monsters and the like outside of the active session. All downtime activities can safely be relegated to out-of-session days - activities like shopping, traveling, researching, investigating, carousing, hiring, scouting, training, and/or conducting class job functions (i.e. assassinations for assassin classes, thieving for thief classes, performances for bard classes, etc). A simple text or email every now and again will allow for players to update their GM as to their characters' activities while not in session.

The method used for tracking time at my table is:

1 ACTUAL DAY = 1 GAME DAY WHEN NO SESSION IS ACTIVE

("1:1 time" going forward) is the easiest, fairest way to determine how time passes within a campaign. Players will have the freedom to conduct any number of activities, several examples of which have been described above, but it is the GM who will be most freed by this rule - the GM will no longer have to make clumsy attempts to describe the passage of time or quickly improvise when the party unexpectedly decides to wait for days or weeks for whatever reason. The GM will be able to fairly determine how territory might shift and change; perhaps they will be able to add granularity to the area with an interesting NPC who happens to be passing through the local village or a group of goblins have moved into a nearby forest and are harassing travelers, for example.

1:1 time divides the game into two separate gameplay types: in-session play and out-of-session play. In-session play is malleable, time can advance as slowly or quickly as the events of the session require. The GM notes how many days have passed in-session as these days must be "made up" in out-of-session play. Out-of-session play is all the days outside of a proper session; these progress at a 1:1 rate and cannot be manipulated forward in time.

An example of the interplay between in-session and out-of-session is as follows: if the party travels for 9 days in session 1...then the GM will note it and time will proceed quickly, skipping to the end of the 9 days. However, by end-of-session, it will be 9 real days before those characters will become available for play again - so if the group gets together 1 day a week then the following session will require them to have alternates, with their traveling characters reaching their destinations 2 days after session 2. The traveling characters will not be able to conduct downtime activities (save for encounters on the road or events like that) while indisposed in this way.

This is illustrated in the chart below:

	Week 1						
	Sunday	Monday	Tuesday	Wednesday	Thursday	Friday	Saturday
IN-GAME	Party begins 9 day journey						
OUT-OF-GAME	Session 1 is conducted						
	Week 2						
	Sunday	Monday	Tuesday	Wednesday	Thursday	Friday	Saturday
IN-GAME			Party arrives at destination				
OUT-OF-GAME	Session 2 is conducted, Session 1 party still on the road.		Party becomes available again				

The chart illustrates how specifically I conduct the passage of time at my own table, though I would note that the above example is rare with actual use of this rule. Players will typically save long periods of travel or downtime for the end of session, preferring to focus on what they can in the moment before the character is temporarily unavailable.

In the event of a dungeon, the party is unlikely to have the option of camping within it without significant preparation of items, supplies, and even personnel. The Dungeon is now an active antagonistic participant (noted here by capitalizing "Dungeon") in the adventure. Games of this type have many methods by which players will be able to leave, even in dire circumstances.

In those few times where my players were intent on clearing the dungeon before the next session but were unable to before the end of the night, they decided to tackle it in-between sessions. The Game Master can sit down and conduct the primary rolls of a dungeon crawl with participating player characters, making sure to keep all involved informed of their progress through the evening; the GM should make sure to clarify things like the percentage of health at which the PCs will retreat and how much they will allow themselves to be encumbered before leaving to consolidate their gains. The Game Master should have copies of all the players' character sheets which they can use to run the adventure. Some players may express trepidation at putting their PCs at risk in this way between sessions...those players ought to return to town at session end; the ones with a higher risk appetite will be just fine, come what may.

The Dungeon will require its own method of time keeping, since there will need to be a way to know how long the party has been down in the depths so that their chances of running into wandering monsters, other adventurers, escaped prisoners, or any other types of encounters can be calculated. This process need not be overly complicated but it is ESSENTIAL toward running a coherent dungeon experience, so it is highly recommended that the GM-Aspirant have some kind of process that is easy to track and gives the players a sense of the passing of time.

In the average campaign where time within the dungeon is not tracked it is common for players to state "I walk here" and they simply move their miniature the distance in the dungeon, stopping only now and again when the GM asks them to make some sort of roll to see whether they spot a trap or not (which often alerts the player that something is wrong). They stride confidently knowing that the beasts that lurk in these forgotten places are static - they do not move from their posts, they do not replenish their numbers.

The players do not fear rival adventurers or appear concerned that the door they intend to check might open before they can reach it. A system to fairly arbitrate the rate at which they explore dungeons will do much to prevent that robotic repetition ("I go here, I check for traps...I go there, I check for traps, I disable the trap...I open the door...").

A system for tracking time progression through the dungeon could work as follows:

1) Exploration turns are tracked in 10 minute chunks of game time.
2) The player characters might only be able to move twice their movement speed in this 10 minute span, representing the PCs taking great care to not trigger traps or attract monsters.
3) In those RPGs with a skill list, where perception and stealth are something rolled for, perhaps the PCs might be able to assume a d20 roll of 10.
4) Some discernment will be required on the part of the Game Master for the number of actions that characters may take since some could be accomplished multiple times and while others will take the full exploration turn to complete.
5) At the end of the exploration turn, the GM will refer to their random encounter table, where they will roll a 1d6; rolling a 1 here means that the party has encountered one of the creatures on their list.

This rule is simple enough to tailor to almost any system and has been enjoyed by my table greatly. The passage of time better establishes the Player Characters' movements through the dungeon and the players are able to more easily conceptualize the feeling of actually being in a dungeon; the movement throughout the Underworld's halls becomes less rote, less "gamey".

Nothing about the actual task of checking for traps has changed practically, but the players suddenly do not mind when the declared action is coupled with the intensity of wondering whether something will emerge from the darkness.

Note that if you decide to use this method, it is highly recommended that the party designate one of their number to be the Caller. This person will be delegated the authority to move the party as they see fit, being that they are playing with friends and their friends trust their decision-making ability. Otherwise, breaking dungeon exploration into individual turns will likely slow the game down as everyone takes their personal movement. Players will of course retain their agency and be able to break off from the Caller's instruction should a description intrigue them or whatever other reason.

Game Masters should consider providing blank graph paper for the party to record the shape and size of rooms, as backtracking through the dungeon can end up taking a large amount of the group's precious time if the dungeon map must be fully recreated around the table in order to visualize its layout. This way, only the relevant areas to the Player Characters' perception must be reconstructed in the case of an event that requires the grid to be depicted in detail.

Having a full map of the Dungeon drawn out this way will also allow incredible locales to be manifested that far exceed the size of the table the players gather around - it will not be necessary to constrain the Dungeon if the overall play area is smaller than the GM would prefer.

ALTERNATIVE PLAY: THEATER OF THE MIND

Theater of the Mind is a method of running exploration and combat around the table that does not require many visual props in order to adjudicate tactical events satisfactorily.

Advantages:
1) Easy setup - nothing beyond the dungeon map on normal graph paper must be drawn.
2) Ease of use - tactics are not required to be meticulously considered.
3) Speed - as the majority of the action is descriptive, combat can be started instantly and ended without requiring cleanup of table-props.

Disadvantages:
1) Lack of visual element - some players are simply more engaged by visual representations of the action.
2) Lack of tactical granularity - actions are declared broadly, perhaps some players may prefer having greater control over the specifics of PC placement and movement.

Exploring the Dungeon will be done in much the same way as described in this chapter, though the primary visual will be the graph paper containing the dungeon map, drawn out as the PCs progress from room to room. If the players have miniatures, these would be arranged on the table to show the marching order of the party and will help inform everyone as to which characters may find themselves targeted in the event of encountering hostile denizens of the Underworld.

Below is an example of Theater of the Mind as played by a group of friends in a campaign run by "Jim the GM":

Say that "Tucker", "Angie", "Rob", and "Jake" are in control of a party of 4 adventurers ambushed by 5 goblins as they round a corner in a dungeon when combat begins...
initiative would be rolled to determine who goes first, then the players would declare their actions -

Tucker: "Mog will charge and attack the first goblin he comes in contact with."
Angie: "Vitelexia will cast Magic Missile, aiming for whichever one looks most in charge."
Jim the GM: "They each look equally combat-hungry, none seem to be ordering the others around."
Angie: "Oh...in that case, she'll target the same one as Mog."
Rob: "Devyn will step in front of Vitelexia and ready an attack against any goblin who comes close"
Jake: "Bollin will try and throw a knife...how far away are they?"
Jim the GM: "The goblins are roughly 20 feet away from you" (the GM points to the squares on the graph paper map the goblins occupy and then to the squares the party occupies) "it's a bit far away and the lighting isn't great...it'll be a tough target."
Jake: "Yeah ok, instead Bollin will try to stick to the shadows and maneuver behind the goblins to sneak attack them."

Note that these fictional players speak broadly as to the actions their characters will take. If a proper map of the Dungeon is being maintained, then they should have a general idea of the size and layout of the battlefield, which is sufficient. If there is some issue with the declared movement or action, then the GM will let the player know what it is or what their character sees, clarifying any confusion; after which the player can adjust their strategy.

At my table, I typically use a mixture of Tactical Play and Theater of the Mind. Sometimes players will end up in hostile encounters unexpectedly and, while enough materials are usually on hand to construct the scene visually, it isn't always worth it to take the time to do so.

A character getting jumped by two thugs in an alleyway, for example, is probably going to be resolved within two rounds one way or the other and is almost definitely going to be straightforward in execution. Players are fine with this, they know as well as you do that all they are going to do is attack and if they want to perform some kind of unorthodox maneuver, they can ask the GM about executing their idea; to which the GM can reply "yea" or "nay".

UTILIZATION OF CHARACTER SKILLS

Skills and skill lists are not so common in rulesets that draw their structure from the systems and mechanics of Old School tabletop RPGs - whereas skill lists are ubiquitous through most modern rules. I would urge caution in the use of skills in the prospective GM's campaign. Skill rolls, in and of themselves, have no merit. Often they are used by GMs to fill time within the session, where they ask the players to roll for trivial things, punishing them for failure on low skill rolls and allowing absurdities for high skill rolls.

The function of the roll is NOT arbitrary...it should always serve a purpose; the skill roll is a method for arbitrating complicated actions with uncertain results; these should not be used for either obviously impossible or obviously trivial tasks. Is a knowledge roll required to guess that the steaming iron cauldrons at the top of the gatehouse is a defensive feature? No, it is obvious!

Another example: a character is well known as a hero about town, having saved the village multiple times over. When this character negotiates at the potion shop for a lower price, perhaps the shopkeeper gives it to him without issue (only making a half-hearted attempt at haggling before acquiescing) and only resorting to a roll if said hero begins to ask for a discount at the limits of the shopkeeper's tolerance. The PC will need to roll to see if he can get more taken off the final price, after a certain point.
Say, instead of a large discount, the player character requests his shopping list to be given to him for free. This will also not require a roll, as the shopkeeper will not part with his goods without payment under any normal circumstances!

The tacit implication of allowing a skill roll is that success is possible and not a waste of time for the player. Rolls made for impossibilities whether allowed to succeed or denied due to their absurdity is a damage to the credibility of the Campaign that accrues over time and with each infraction.

ENCUMBRANCE & LOOT

It is a common choice among GMs that they do not bother with aspects of the game involving weight or encumbrance. Parties haul about hundreds of thousands of coins without penalty and easily carry out all the equipment in a dungeon, for fear of the paperwork involved with keeping track of such things.

This is a mistake.

Determining what to grab and how much to carry is as important to the game as leveling up or slaying monsters. Two methods are available to the GM aspirant:
1) Players track their carried weight individually, noting when they are encumbered
2) A player is given the job of tracking the party loot bag and equipment carried (the Quartermaster), encumbrance is tracked as a matter of the group combined strength scores

I have found that option 2 worked quite well while the players became accustomed to not being able to grab everything they could touch. Option 1 is where the table ended up, as they slowly became irritated by sharing carry capacity with lower strength PCs, however the job of Quartermaster remained so as to minimize the confusion of who is carrying what.

In the interest of keeping the game moving and reducing the pain of suddenly enforcing this rule, all weight had been converted from pounds to "slots" - with a slot consisting of roughly 5 lbs of items and then listing out as many item types as possible, so that the whole equipment list might be represented in a single chart, the intention is to reduce the necessity of returning to the core rulebooks for specific to-the-fraction accounting of total weight carried by handing the example chart for players to keep a copy of in their binders:

Equipment Weight Table

Equipment	Weight in Slots
Light Armor:	4
Medium Armor:	7
Heavy Armor:	10
Light Shield:	1
Heavy Shield:	2
Tower Shield:	3
Ammunition (50)	1
1H Melee Weapon:	1
2H Melee Weapon:	2
Bow:	1
Light Crossbow	1
Crossbow:	2
Belt (5):	1
Amulet (5):	1
Potions (10):	1
Scrolls (20):	1
Adventuring Gear (5)*:	1
Bedroll:	1
Small Tent:	4
Medium Tent:	6
Large Tent:	8
Pavilion Tent:	10
Coins (100):	1

* adventuring gear includes daggers/knives, rations, hygiene products, holy symbols, and various knick-knacks commonly found on adventurers

The observant reader will notice that COINS HAVE WEIGHT. This promises to be controversial with many groups, but it is essential that limits be placed upon the ability of characters to haul things out of the dungeon; I compromise on this by allowing the weight of coins to be generously small, though this isn't necessary, and some would argue should be much harsher! It should be suggested to players who struggle with this to consider the hiring of NPCs to haul their loot for them - with the PCs taking care to protect their hirelings, lest they find it difficult to hire more if they should acquire a reputation as dangerous employers.

You may be surprised to find that the players become attached to the NPCs they hire in this way. It helps them feel like they're living in the world that you have created and the men and women they meet may end up becoming Player Characters themselves one day.

EXPERIENCE AWARDS & LEVEL GROWTH

Tabletop RPGs are defined by mechanics like classes, levels, combat, and loot - therefore it is necessary to examine the assumptions we make with regard to the gaining of experience and levels. Often the modern method relies on a "Checkpoint System" where character levels are awarded for completing certain plotted story events, these levels are usually given to all players simultaneously, regardless of attendance. A Living Campaign cannot function at its best this way, as the story and pace are set by the characters and their willingness to invest time and resources into their interests and the game as a whole. As such the players need to rely on the more traditional system of Experience Point awards (also abbreviated as "XP").

There are many ways to go about bequeathing this enigmatic resource to players, but the method that I hold to be the best is:
1 Gold Piece secured through adventuring = 1 Experience Point
Player Characters awarded XP for the procurement of monetary rewards is a profoundly fair method of discerning what a PC is entitled to with regard to the growth of their abilities and encourages them to explore and always push forward in search of more treasure that will further drive the expansion of their power and talents.

The most common application of this method only awards XP for the slaying of monsters or is arbitrarily awarded at the GM's discretion for the completing of quests. It is my sincere belief that XP awards of 1 gold piece = 1 experience point is necessary to create a complete gaming experience -

otherwise players are incentivized to cause as much mayhem as possible as they slay monsters and men alike and/or the GM doles out the XP too reluctantly (or too generously).

XP ought to be awarded asymmetrically, to incentivize player attendance and to adjudicate rewards fairly. Players can allocate larger shares of gold loot to others who missed the previous sessions if they would like to help them catch up.

The idea that players are unduly punished for being occasionally unable to make attendance is largely overblown; they are unlikely to fall too far behind due to the occasional lapse in presence and it is even less likely others will have a perfect record themselves.

In addition to strict coin, XP ought to be awarded for the monetary value of any equipment procured by the players. These items may not be gold pieces in the strictest sense, they are still very valuable and great skill was likely used in the process of their procurement. On its face, this seems to enable a mechanic that players could easily abuse to grow character levels with incredible speed...a result that would indeed damage player immersion (even if they themselves would argue that it's fine) should it be implemented without the appropriate caveats.

First, XP awards ought to be capped at the threshold for a PC's next class level up, with any excess XP value lost. Players will still enjoy the benefits of a large payday, but their training and growth will continue at an acceptable pace that is more easily manageable for the GM and player. Second, Player Characters should be required to pay high monetary costs and spend time to complete the process of leveling up; expensive training costs will help regulate the PC's income and encourage them to always keep adventuring to be better able to pay for their next level and still afford new equipment, when the time comes.

To be specific, I use the following rule to determine the criteria around a character's leveling up in common d20 systems:

GAINING EXPERIENCE LEVELS

Gaining the experience points (XP) required to level up does not automatically make a character more powerful. A period of training and study is required to fully utilize the experience gained in the previous adventures.

The length of this period will be determined by how a Player Character performed as a member of their class. Does the Fighter refuse to be the vanguard for fear of potential injury? Then they will likely need to spend more time pondering the nature of their class and ridding themselves of their cowardice.

Upon leveling up, Player Characters will be evaluated by the Game Master (GM):
E - Excellent: performed to the specifications of their class (1)
S - Superior: minor deviations from class function but otherwise performed to expectations (2)
F - Fair: significant deviation, but still largely performed to class and alignment (3)
P - Poor: aberrant behavior, entirely failed to fulfill class function or character alignment (4)

Upon completion of each adventure, the above ratings will be assigned to each Player Character. The average of the ratings will reveal a number between 1 and 4 - this is the number of weeks required to gain a level.

COST OF LEVELING UP

Between levels 1 and 10, a Player Character will refer to the following formula for costs associated with leveling ("Level of Character" referring to the current level of the character, not the level to be gained):

"LEVEL OF CHARACTER X 1,000 = WEEKLY COST DURING STUDY/TRAINING"

A Player Character between levels 1 and 10 must find a trainer. A barbarian must learn from a barbarian, an inquisitor must learn from an inquisitor, etc. A Player Character who achieves an Excellent (1) rating may opt instead to study on their own, though the time spent will be doubled to 2 weeks.

Upon achieving level 10, a Player Character is considered an elite member of his or her class. They are no longer required to find a trainer and are fully capable of self-study regardless of performance rating. At this point, leveling costs will be determined by class:

Full Divine Caster = 1,500/level/week (vestments & largess)
Full Martial Class = 600/level/week (tithes & largess)
Full Arcane Caster = 3,000/level/week (equipment, books, experiments, etc.)
Skilled Class/Partial Caster = 1,500/level/week (tools, equipment, etc.)

A Player Character that has reached the minimum requirement for advancement is no longer awarded XP until the new level is actually gained.

The reader will notice that according to the above rules errata, the GM grades the performance of the players with regard to their class function and alignment; this is mechanically designed to weed out players who would fail to function as a member of the party and helps encourage them to act within the game in-character per their role. It is up to the GM what they would classify as an "adventure" per the above, but it need not be overly meticulous. It is enough to have a general idea of a character's recent performance when assigning their grade, just be ready to defend it if it is higher than 1!

Trainers will function as mentors and allies to their students. These are excellent opportunities to introduce an NPC from a player character's background associations and help them move along their personal trajectory. They can also be new characters unrelated to the current party! Meeting people is part of living somewhere, after all. An important side effect of the imposition of training times creates what could informally be called "Level Up Jail" where the PC in the process of achieving the next level will be unavailable for adventures or other downtime activities.

The player should be encouraged to take on a new PC while they wait. Too much thought regarding the exact amount of XP to award in a session is counterproductive to the efficient running of the Campaign. If the above criteria for handling player character leveling is followed and the players are bound by 1:1 time, the GM will find that the players may reach the threshold for the next level but find themselves unable or unwilling to go back to town immediately in order to find a trainer and thereby lose a week of adventuring.

If they leave the dungeon incompletely looted, it creates the risk that other adventuring groups, raiders, bandits, and/or other monsters will be able seize the remaining treasure out from under the PC's noses...so losing control of a character following the session might be more trouble than it is worth to the player and they may defer leveling up for the time being.

Whatever happens makes no difference to the GM - either way, the character has been limited in the accumulation of XP so as not to grow too quickly and the player gets to make real decisions about how their PC will interact with the world.

THE CAMPAIGN GROWS

You will find the longer that you run a campaign with this method, the more established PCs will become in the world. At my table, for example, a PC has acquired a keep where he has begun the task of searching for missing children from his village. The keep comes with a lordship, a small hamlet, natural resources, a community of neutral wood elves, and a roaming band of orcs who use the heavy forest to hide from reprisal, along with a number of dungeons yet unexplored by intrepid adventurers. He has established roads, defensive fortifications, and begun to raise mercenaries and soldiers to defend his keep and the people immediately surrounding. Naturally, he draws an income from the production and sale of natural resources; he has drawn the expensive attentions of both his new liege-lord and the Church.

As far as assigning value to resources or the tax rate, the Foundational Ruleset should have the costs of commodities within its pages that will help inform the GM-Aspirant as to what the value of the land's contents should be. Some players may end up with incredible resources at their disposal, but between level-up costs, purchasing new equipment, fortifying holdings, and dealing with emergent threats...it will take a truly enormous recurring sum to remove that hunger for more gold from their bellies.

The PC in the above example takes a draw of the keep income at the end of each real world month less the taxes and expenses associated with running the hex. He makes decisions and issues decrees as ideas strike him, he sends a message with the specifics where I can take my time to deliberate and consider the appropriate ruling on such things. None of this impacts the experience of the other players, who are happy to inquire about the downtime activities of their own.

Higher level PCs will become mentors and quest-givers for fellow player's lower level PCs. An entire system of patronage existing within a single play group can emerge...perhaps Rob's level 5 Fighter swears loyalty to Angie's Level 12 Cleric or Jake's level 8 Rogue hires Tucker's level 4 Bard to run a distraction while he attempts to swindle the local guardhouse.

Do not be afraid to set a decent tax rate and any number of fees, this will irritate the participating player or otherwise provide an opportunity for them to really get into the character of a lordling. It is even appropriate to take 20% to 40% of a player's recurring income as many individuals might attempt to get their hands in the cookie jar of their lord's wallet.

This is an undeniably complex set of connections and situations that would be near impossible to run without the use of 1:1 time. Running in-depth scenarios involving only a single PC, all within the session, would bore the other players to tears - their stake in these events would be small. With the days between sessions being fair game: downtime activity spent on the maintenance of holdings can be arbitrated by the GM at their leisure in the days leading up to the next game night.

It is in the common method of freezing time between sessions that requires the most work on the part of the GM: by barring themselves and their players from the time that exists outside the session, their arbitrations will necessarily *have* to be made right there at the table, within that evening, since the player characters are not able to act with time so frozen when the session ends. This is especially grueling if the GM is arbitrating some personal event for a single Player Character while the other players look on and patiently await the resumption of the game for themselves!

The prospective GM might be intimidated by what has been described so far, but these are the fruits of their initial work: the Campaign has begun to produce narratives spontaneously!
Refer to the enormous body of content online that describes the processes that "successful" GMs participate in - it is a significantly more complicated endeavor to attempt to anticipate the myriad avenues of activity a group of players may go to from session to session. Game Master Burnout is a real phenomenon and the reason is because enormous amounts of planning time is required, lest the players begin to glimpse the man behind the curtain. A Living Campaign will only require the occasional roll of the dice to see if groups of monsters have moved into player-occupied territory or if NPCs have begun to make moves into the active play area of the Campaign.

These do not need to always be random rolls, occasionally it might be easier to will it so by fiat in those situations where the potential event makes sense; rolling on a table or within some arbitrary value is the method that the GM uses to outsource their decision-making on things they are unsure of, simply abdicating to the dice whether or not an NPC makes a certain decision.

APPROACHING MASS COMBAT

Mass combat is an aspect of the game that has a significant likelihood of occuring at advanced tables and represents the highest stage of campaign development: that of the Domain. It is certainly unlikely new players will engage with such things at the outset, but eventually one or more will gravitate toward the training and commanding of PC-lead armies if the campaign is conducted as instructed thus far. Often armies can, and will, engage one another in out-of-session play and the results can be arbitrated by the GM or players sometime before the next session (assuming the use of 1:1 time). Players may decide that a character needs to be at the head of a fighting force IN-SESSION and the GM would be well served to be prepared for that eventuality.

The contemporary methods of executing mass combat usually involve trying to hand-wave the larger conflict away due to the cumbersome number of individuals or attempt to turn the battle into a large set-piece where the players zip around the field, trying to accomplish objectives while slogging their way through several consecutive combat encounters. The battle in this instance occurs as background decoration, with soldiers being *described* as fighting one another but with no dice or mechanical engagement to speak of; the outcome of the struggle hinges on objectives that were defined by some NPC or the GM in an expositive piece. This is a nightmare to plan (as well as rarely being fun for players), as I have run several large scale "battles" in this way and have participated in such struggles as a player in the past.

It is sound advice to an aspiring GM to consider the ruleset that they have selected.

The method I use is simple:

Scale up the skirmish combat rules of the foundational ruleset to a 1:10 scale. That is: 1 action for every 10 combatants in the mass battle. The movements, time passed per round, damage rolled, etc. are all likewise scaled upward by a factor of 10. It is well-trod territory to remark that the most well-known tabletop RPG in the world was derived from the Man-to-Man Combat rules of Chainmail - written by Gary Gygax and Jeff Perren. Much of the ability scores and statistics of contemporary games likewise share a mechanical lineage with wargames and will remain coherent up to a certain scale.

It is usually the case that the actions taken in combat at the skirmish layer can remain sensical at the mass battle layer. A charge remains a charge, a defensive action remains a defensive action, etc. Some Tabletop RPGs are better for this than others; the reader should acquaint themselves with the specifics of the combat mechanics of the ruleset they have chosen and see for themselves if those rules remain viable when they are scaled up to include groups acting in cohesion rather than a single hero character acting on their own. Devising a method to scale up combat in this way will require some intuition as well as trial and error on the GM's part. It is best to maintain "normal combat, but bigger" as True North when conceptualizing mass combat in a typical TTRPG ruleset - the scaled version of the base game's existing combat mechanics will almost assuredly be more fun than whatever supplemental system has been bolted on by such-and-such book of the chosen ruleset.

It should be emphasized that this subject is HIGHLY unlikely to occur for AT LEAST several real-world months after beginning the Campaign. Whether or not the prospective GM has fully comprehended the idea of mass combat should have no bearing on the arrival of the first session. Mastery over the game comes with actually playing...and that mastery will provide the confidence to tackle any number of complicated subjects.

A few best practices for mass combat:
1) Tie the initiative order solely between commanders, so that one whole side goes at a time.
2) Begin on a x10 scale, with up to 40 or 50 units per square or per inch; every ten soldiers receives an attack roll and a damage roll on a hit.
3) Damage should scale by the number of soldiers in the group; 10 soldiers will multiply damage by 10 on a hit, 26 soldiers will receive 3 attacks (1st = 10 soldiers, 2nd = 10 soldiers, 3rd = 6 soldiers; total: 26); the 3rd attack will only multiply damage by 6 in this example.
4) Damage received should be divided by the max value of the damaged soldier type's hit die (the type of dice rolled for hp at level up).
5) Hit die are a measure of the relative durability and experience of a character or creature (literally the number of times they can be hit). A warrior unit that receives 250 points of damage from a cavalry charge may have two d10 hit die; 250 / 10 = 25 soldiers received 1 hit die of damage - 25 of 26 will be reduced to 1 hit die with 1 unharmed. Another hit like that and many soldiers could be devastated!

6) Damage should circulate throughout the unit, allowing hundreds of soldiers to focus all of their carnage upon one soldier of many in a block of bodies is rather unreasonable in a chaotic battlefield situation.

EXAMPLE DUNGEON: GROTTO OF THE WINTER CIRCLE
FOUNDATIONAL RULES: PATHFINDER 1ST ED.

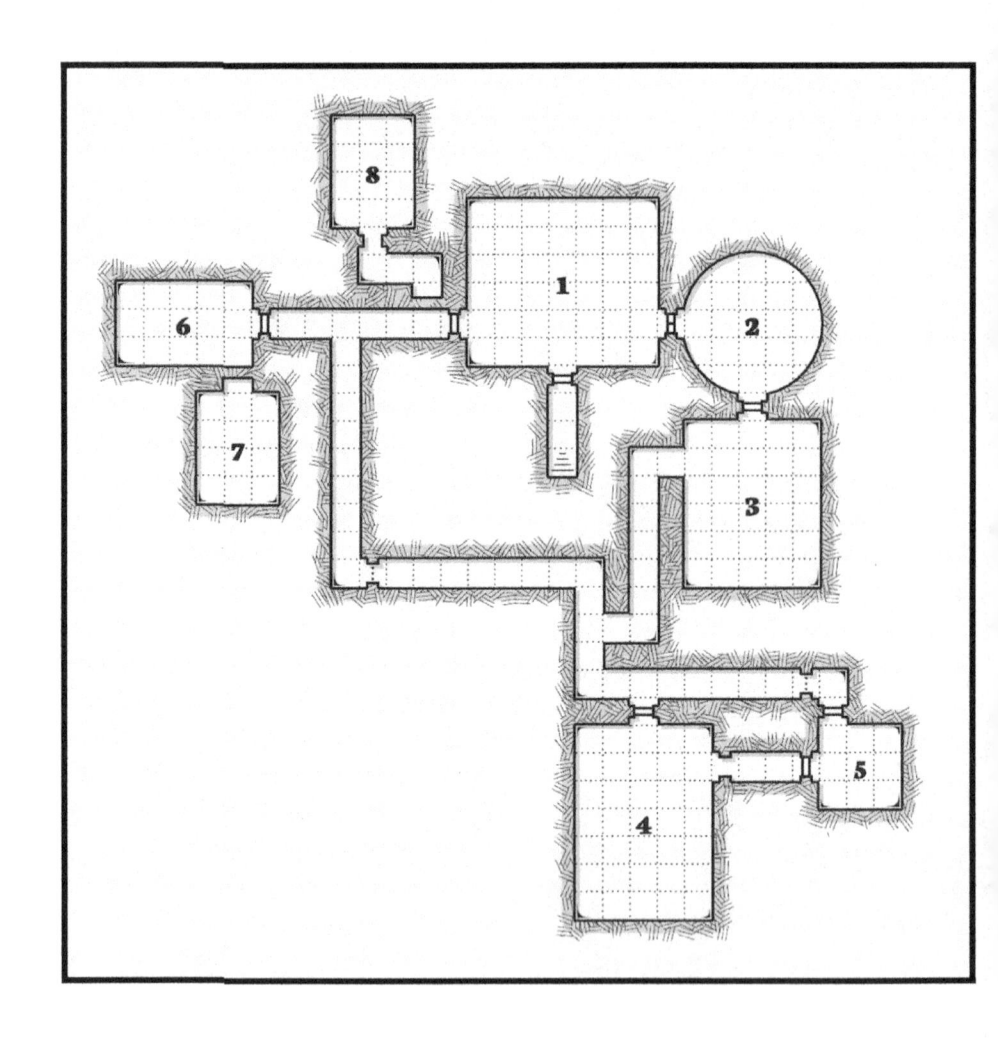

Lvl: 2
Location:
Found By:

Floor 1:

1-1 (trap): **Fey Hall** - this room has 2 mid-sized trees without leaves. The temperature feels seasonally appropriate, though snow is on the ground. Something about this place feels open, as though you are NOT beneath the ground.

Frostbite Trap: Perception DC 27; Disable Device DC 27
Trigger: non-fey opening the left door
Effect: spell effect (acid arrow, but cold dmg, Atk +2 ranged touch, 2d4 cold dmg for 4 rounds)

1-2: **Dance Hall** - a circular stage can easily be seen from anywhere in the room. Seats of twisted brambles and tree stumps are intermittently placed

1-3 (encounter): **Winter Court Hall** - wooden armor, winter plants, and more snow decorate this room, making it seem a smaller version of a Damoclesian court chamber.
Encounter: 4 wolves (400 XP each)

1-4 (locked, trap, treasure): **First World Armory** - the door to this room is locked; it contains weapons and armor that look almost like art pieces.
Locked: North Door - Disable Device DC 22
Burning Hands Trap: Perception DC 25; Disable Device DC 25
Trigger: opening the door after unlocking
Effect spell effect (burning hands, 4d4 fire dmg, Ref save DC 13 for half dmg); all targets in 15 ft. cone-shaped burst
Treasure: 8,515 sp; 1 chain shirt +1 (1,250 XP), 1 studded leather armor +1 (1,175 XP), 1 leather armor +2 (4,160 XP), 1 silver shock warhammer +1 (8,402 XP), 1 light crossbow +2 (8,335 XP), 1 huntsman dagger +1 (8,302 XP)

1-5 (trick, hint): **Rune Control Room** - 4 colored runes are lined up against the east wall. Nothing else seems to be in this room. On the ceiling, 4 large snowflakes are spaced evenly on the blue ceiling.
Trick: Colors correspond to the seasons. They are in this order on the wall from left to right:
 1) Green
 2) Yellow
 3) Red
 4) Blue
Touching blue 4 times will cause the light of the rune to glow progressively brighter and the glow of the others will get dimmer. On the 4th touch, the path to room 1-8 opens.

Touching them in this order: Blue -> Yellow -> Green -> Red causes room 1-7 to open; this is symbolic of Winter being the first among the seasons, then Fall as it leads to Winter, then Spring as it emerges from Winter, with Summer last - Summer is the great enemy of Winter since these seasons do not touch.

1-6 (encounter): **Winter Landscape** - this room almost seems to be outside, the air is chilled and light illuminates the sun in the sky. You squint, only to realize that the scenery is a mere painting mixed with lifelike carving: it depicts an elf-like figure standing proudly atop a tall hill, clad in ice-blue armor. A breathtakingly beautiful woman watches him longingly; her long, flowing dress a mixture of yellow and orange, a pile of colored leaves lay scattered at her feet. A child looks to be climbing from the base of the hill, he totters upward, unsteady on his feet. In the valley below the three, a black-iron knight holds a torch; his eyes are contorted with hatred as he stares up at the blue-armored fae warrior.

Encounter: 5 hobgoblins (200 XP each)

1-7 (secret, treasure): **Golden Treasury** - an open chest with a pile of gold coins overflowing from it spills onto the floor. The image from room 1-6 completes the story as the blue warrior is united with his lover and his child, the red knight lay slain on the field of battle.

Treasure: 4,572 gp (4,572 XP)

1-8 (secret, treasure): **Platinum Treasury** - a similar sized chest sits open, a pile of platinum coins beckons.

Treasure: 862 pp (8,620 XP)

ENCOUNTER TABLE:

Every 10 min: roll 1d6; roll of "1" = encounter

Floor 1:
1d6 - encounter creature on # rolled;
1) 3 hobgoblins
2) 1 dire rat, 3 dire rats, 1 dire rat (animal)
3) 4 skeletons (mindless)
4) 4 bandits, 6 bandits
5) 6 goblins
6) 5 orcs, 4 orcs

Disposition:
Base 50% + Charisma Modifier: +5% per +1 modifier (or -5% per -1 modifier) + Outsider Penalty: -35%
Succeed More Than 20% = friendly/willing to help; 0% = neutral; Fail More Than 10% = hostile

PART II

DEFENDING THE METHOD

The recommendations contained within this work were not spontaneously generated by myself; but are a result of the compiled wisdom of the roleplayers and wargamers that have come before - in addition to my own personal experience running campaigns of many types in varied rules systems. *The Living Campaign* is an attempt to extract a blanket set of assumptions and objectives from the systems and styles of play from an earlier epoch and translate them for the more ambitious players and game masters of the current year. The suggestions contained here can be placed over many current, in-use Tabletop RPGs - their implementation is intended to create a rich and fulfilling experience across as many tables as possible for the greatest number of players.

The original conceptualization of Tabletop RPGs was derived from the Minnesota wargames culture that produced figures like Gary Gygax and Dave Arneson. They themselves would have been influenced by the British wargames culture of names like Tony Bath and Don Featherstone, who were active in the preceding decade. In the wargames campaign instructional book, *Tony Bath's Ancient Wargaming*, Bath describes the set up of his long-running Hyborian Campaign; the descriptions and methods that he employs are conceptually similar to the methods that Gygax would recommend in his own Dungeon Master's Guide several years later. As time has gone on, these roots have slowly been overwritten, but many of the mechanics Gygax and Arneson laid out would survive into future editions and spin-off RPGs.

It is unfortunate that the rules systems contained in these descendant RPGs are a struggle to implement for many who attempt them - a consequence of the instructions guiding their use often being disconnected from the original assumptions surrounding TTRPGs from when they were first implemented. The game designers from that era took for granted what the players and referees of their games would understand about their creations and, as such, the rules they laid down can seem almost incomprehensibly strange to the readers of *this* era.

For those that are skeptical about the effectiveness of my description of the role of the Dungeon, time tracking in 1:1, or other such recommendations: this section is intended to help assuage doubts and aid the reader in gleaning the purpose of some of the aforementioned injunctions that guide the running of my own ongoing campaign.

Contemporary methods for building a campaign are often insufficient in accomplishing their stated goal of a fun, long-term game with regular attendance. While certain talented individuals of unusually large imagination are able to succeed and create long-running campaigns that players remember fondly, it is far too common to hear stories among friends and acquaintances of being subjected to gross boredoms and social terrors. In fact, these stories are so ubiquitous through the community that one may wonder if the accepted implementation of the rules and various pieces of received wisdom *themselves* induce a campaign into collapse.

Now it seems that several gaming tables make claims to be able to maintain a regular campaign for a significant length of time using the modern methods of game design and they are perfectly content to continue to do so. These are often more theater-oriented tables where the players delight in improvisational roleplay and the GM serves their game by performing the "yes and" role to the players' actions. The rolling dice and attacking monsters is also plenty of fun between sincerely acted out character scenes.

The concern that I have is that the vast majority of instruction that is currently in circulation seems to exist purely to create these sorts of gaming tables. This style of game is an excellent fit for a very specific type of person and seems a sub-optimal fit for everyone else, one must only scroll through the many purveyors of tabletop horror stories and their endless streams of content, their overall popularity, and the desperate lack of available Game Masters that permit the deranged to help create these stories in the first place to understand that perhaps there is a deep rooted problem in the conventional wisdom surrounding campaign creation.

The entire premise of this work rests on the assumption that the issues plaguing these tables can be mitigated or altogether eliminated through rules and mechanics. I believe that what most players and GMs suffer from is ultimately an engineering issue and that some adjustment to their a priori beliefs about the best way to play the game will do positive things for many campaigns and hopefully help alleviate the lack of quality tables.

THE CASE FOR A MECHANICAL FOUNDATION

The days of the hobby being under a single systems umbrella are more or less over. For better or for worse no two tables are remotely alike; even from those Game Masters who learned together, their styles will differ significantly. For those seeking to enter the hobby this is an affecting, irritating, and sometimes horrifying problem.

Horror stories abound about new players' first experience with the game where they had someone's twisted imagination or petty megalomania inflicted upon them. It is clear that the hobby suffers from having no unifying vision about what the game could, or should, be and so newcomers don't have a serious idea of what to expect when joining a game for the first time.

The Mechanical Foundation allows for the existence of other systems; the instruction provided attempts to establish a governing mindset to create commonality of function between tables regardless of whether or not those tables use the same core rulebooks.

For the amateur GM the establishment of an early mindset will inform the running of their tables as they approach mechanical mastery of their chosen system. Whether the campaign lives or dies is a reflection of whichever philosophy guides the running of the table.

Broad adoption of like methods between gaming groups such as 1:1 time, encumbrance tracking, the creation of original campaign settings, and leveling costs will create a common etiquette where players will more easily be able to move from table to table while still maintaining some sense of continuity with their previous experiences...even if those new tables do not use the ruleset more familiar to the player, they will still be able to understand what is expected of them and what they can expect from the Game Master. "Understanding Expectations" is a key component for achieving harmony between all involved parties - logically, *some* uniformity between tables helps create a network of readily available players and GMs that can assume that any associated party will be able to fall in with the others without major issue.

The above advice *excludes* games that do not involve adventures, dice rolls, the procurement of loot and treasure, or are otherwise aiming for altogether different experience. I am not interested in scolding long established groups that have a method they are well practiced in: I am only concerned with providing an accessible alternative to the advice that the frustrated GM has received thus far.

CREATE ONLY WHAT IS NECESSARY: NON-PLAYER CHARACTERS

Not all NPCs will be equally valuable to the Campaign; the vast majority of the characters in proximity to the player characters will be townsfolk going about their lives; should the GM be expected to establish the personalities of every single villager? It would be a misallocation of mental and chronological resources to become overly fixated on individuals the Player Characters may never encounter or care to engage with again. Strong efforts to create memorable non-player characters that are casually dismissed can cause a great deal of inner turmoil in the Game Master and is no doubt a contributor to burnout. It hurts the long term viability of a campaign any time hours of work are laid to rest without generating AT LEAST as much time in play around the table.

That said, those that the party will NEED to interact with ought to be well-developed. Any community will have its movers and shakers, it is no great crime of laziness to focus only on the prominent individuals, and their families, in a large town or city. Caution is advised against the temptation to introduce an *over-designed* NPC: the GM plots an elaborate background, ties them in meticulously with several PCs and factions, and gives them grand motivations only to realize that all this work would be wasted should the party refuse to take them on. Many hours of work have been lost when players indeed refuse their help!

Mastery over the creation and implementation of non-player characters has a learning curve, but learning it will ultimately reduce the overall work required in the planning and maintaining of the Campaign.

This should be the main question the GM asks themselves when creating NPCs: "will this increase or decrease the amount of time I spend planning for the next session?"

An exception can be made as needed, perhaps the prospective GM simply enjoys roleplaying random characters? By all means create and run them! What is the point of saving time if the GM can't spend it on the parts of their setting that they personally enjoy?

The instructions for creating NPC characters are based on the principle that limited time and resources ought to be applied to where they are needed the most. While this might be regarded as obvious by the reader, it does need to be stated frankly; it is perfectly possible for even well-practiced and professional people to become fixated on aspects of a project that have a limited impact on the overall outcome of that project; this is as true in tabletop campaigns as it is in school or work.

The creation of NPCs can trap GMs in a single stage of their planning, so it should be kept in their minds that they need to ask themselves if certain less-than-important NPCs are taking too much of the GM's limited planning time...and then save their energy for those characters that absolutely require it. Perhaps they ought to focus on NPCs integral to the backgrounds of the player characters, where deficiencies are far more likely to be noticed and noted by the players when they are encountered, for example.

The NPCs will then need to populate a world...but what should the world they live in be like? How do we create/run something that players will enjoy?

HOW TO CREATE A WORLD

Four significant declarations are made in this chapter:
- Societies based on real world or existing fictional cultures are preferable
- Ecological accuracy is NOT necessary
- Knowing the location and type of natural resources is good
- It is best to begin in a borderland

SOCIETIES BASED ON REAL WORLD OR ESTABLISHED FICTIONAL HISTORIES ARE PREFERABLE

It is perfectly acceptable to apply real world societies and factions for use within a campaign setting; a GM can blend history together to create something at once new and familiar. It is my impression that there is an entrenched fear of being derivative within the hobby - a fear which seems largely misplaced as players can easily become attached to even the most familiar genre settings so long as they are able to leave their mark upon it - I have run contiguous campaigns in the same setting in a single nation derived almost exclusively from 9th and 11th century Britain for over 10 years and players have never hesitated to return or complained of boredom.

Beyond the aesthetic trappings of what is commonly known about medieval life, history has a deep and abiding richness embedded within it that many people have not a clue about. It is useful that lightly skimming readily available articles with a focus on such subjects will provide the GM-Aspirant with fertile ground upon which to build their own unique nation. Even a cursory dive will yield details that can be used to build a campaign setting that possesses a familiarity that allows players to get their bearings, yet will remain alien enough so that they will not easily be able to predict its workings.

This is the primary advantage in adapting real world societal structures and norms into a campaign setting: a borrowed realness and inexhaustible resources through which new details and data can be drawn. This method of drafting a setting is closed to the Game Master who insists on creating something completely original. It should also be noted, that real history is not the only method of creation that is available to the GM: it is no faux pas to borrow aesthetics, names, and structures from existing media of any type and transplant them into your game wholesale, if need be. The GM does not need to take on the responsibility of a producer or director in addition to their primary duties - they simply need to designate the play area that the players will interact with. If this play area is pulled from a favorite book series or television show makes no difference: so long as it is consistent with regard to itself, it will be playable just the same.

ECOLOGICAL ACCURACY IS NOT NECESSARY

Do not let the perfect become the enemy of the good! How many games, books, or screenplays fail to be born due to some misplaced notion that everything must be realistically accurate or wholly consistent? Many forms of media are left unfinished as their would-be creators tweak and alter and edit and rebuild over and over and over, the finished product (or the first page of the story!) never arrives; the setting is not yet perfect and the story cannot begin until it achieves that perfection!

No, the GM's number one job is to GET THE GAME GOING. All but the most egregious inconsistencies are highly unlikely to be noticed and in the event that they are noticed: a simple shrug and a smile might inspire a player to create a character that wants to uncover the mysteries of such a strange, unexplained phenomena.

KNOWING THE LOCATION AND TYPE OF NATURAL RESOURCES IS GOOD

The instinct is to scoff at taking the time to figure out what is considered to be an uninteresting mundanity. It would behoove the skeptical reader to consider that interesting quirks of geological formations have a significant impact on the regions where they are located here in the real world. Is it actually so boring to see a certain "character" of the world begin to emerge as these things are placed upon the land? It is knowing the particulars of the regions of a country that will serve the Game Master GREATLY when their players arrive in new areas and explore the land.

The players are chasing a quality called "immersion", a quality that makes them feel connected to the setting; what they see and the people they interact with will largely be influenced by the local economy. Arriving in a new town inevitably leads to descriptions of the shops, stalls, foods, decorations, etc. and all of these things can either be recorded arbitrarily, which requires a great deal of dedication to not lead to strange inconsistencies that sharp players will notice, or they can be determined by knowing the basic economy of the area through some method of random rolling that can be accomplished in a few minutes.

The method is not required to be complicated and the result is not required to be overly detailed, knowing the area in broad strokes ought to be enough to keep the creative fires burning. Details expounded to the players through randomly generated prompts merely require a note so that the GM will be able to remember what they declared for future reference.

IT IS BEST TO BEGIN IN A BORDERLAND

When playing in a brand new campaign setting for the first time, there may be an impulse to release players into a sprawling metropolis or a likewise stable polity deep within the well-regulated borders of a nation. This is not advised for a new campaign, since both the GM and the Players will be inexperienced at the outset, and the lack of obvious problems may stymie their decision-making as they aren't sure how to go about finding something to do. My preferred solution would be to begin the game in a frontier bordertown, which has several advantages for GMs and Players. The border to uncharted wilderness eases players into the particulars of the realm that holds their adventures; learning about how the township functions, what challenges they face, and accruing valuable contacts along with gainful employment are the primary aspects of the start of a campaign. The borders of civilization carry a mythical quality that suggests monsters, caves, ruins, and most importantly: treasure.

It is a mysterious place where rumors swirl and people huddle around their fires against the surrounding darkness. Adventurers are free to operate as they see fit, since the proper authorities are either lightly represented or not present at all (hence the need for adventurers). It simply isn't the case that the GM needs to be the one to "hook" players into actually playing the game: they only need to provide an avenue for the accrual of strength and wealth and then it is up to the players themselves to decide what the point of their adventuring is. Large cities are where the players will go when their characters begin to grow in scope, when they need a patron or henchmen. The city is for the expansion of social bonds, more expensive equipment, or the pursuit of personal goals unrelated to the act of adventuring - all of these are unnecessary for Player Characters at the start of a campaign.

WHY TO CREATE A WORLD

With the proliferation of published modules the Game Master might be wondering why they should even bother with the creation of a setting of their own, since building one's own "homebrew" campaign requires consistent work from the individual in the beginning of its creation and the GM-Aspirant may not view themselves as particularly creative; would it not make sense to outsource such things to books and modules already written?

This is certainly a legitimate concern to have when one does not have practiced experience to lean on...however, to refer exclusively to a pre-written setting is a great disservice to oneself! Through playing the game, there will come a time when the world ceases to be the sole possession of only the GM, but also of the players. Such a world uniquely belongs to the table of its origin, to see it grow and breathe is as though the creation has truly come to life.

Even a world designed by an absolute creative novice will have appeal to the people around the table: after all, everything that happens and the people they meet are theirs and theirs alone. Modules, conversely, can be experienced multiple times by GM and Player - leading to awkward moments where players might join a game running a module they've already experienced. In those cases that player will discover where various details were altered and may experience frustration when some outcomes are identical to what they've experienced while others change for reasons unknown. A Living Campaign has the ultimate advantage as it marches ever forward through time - players will drop out, they will join up, they could be new or veteran...but they will never repeat sessions upon sessions worth of content ever again.

APPLIED CHAOS IS A POWERFUL TOOL

Random tables occupy a strange space in the consciousness of the tabletop enthusiast. It is common to see posts or threads on the internet or in publications where elaborate tables are shown off to the digital cheers of the crowd, but then I have never seen CONSISTENT use of these tables in my long history as a GM, being involved with tabletop RPGs since the mid-2000s - these homebrewed tables would be celebrated and then immediately forgotten.

The common perception of tools like the random encounter table at the time, for example, is that they slowed the game down to an interminable crawl as the dice called more monsters to the fight. The advice from many sources was that the GM ought to exercise caution when using random tables so the players would not get bored. They were considered a last resort to get a slow party moving or an incentive to stop lollygagging in a hostile area and even then, their use came with many caveats. It seems their inclusion in derivative systems and rulesets was almost a vestigial habit of publishing.

The random table's original conception and intended use is NOT correctly described in the above.

Random tables of all types are best conceived of as tools designed for a specific purpose - each has the situation they are best used in and each has a proper way to go about being handled so that they succeed in enhancing the game. The common function of all random tables is to make decisions for the GM that would otherwise be too difficult to parse quickly or are too complex relative to their impact on the overall session and the player characters.

For example, the random encounter table for a dungeon serves the GM by making the decision about when a creature is encountered and then deciding what type of creature makes contact with the Party, either hostile or friendly. Should the GM take the time to make individual decisions for every creature in an area in real time, assessing their approximate location with only the source map and their notes for guidance?

No, it is far easier and suitably organic to simplify the issue down to rolling once to see if a monster is encountered and once more to determine whether or not they are immediately hostile. The GM's mental endurance is a finite resource within a session and ought to be conserved for those times when serious thought is required; it would be wasted and the evening would be unacceptably slowed as dozens of monsters would need to be moved individually. The more readily accepted alternative solution is to have monsters simply milling about in rooms, waiting for the arrival of the PCs...yet doing so renders the Dungeon a static place - preserving the mental stamina of the GM comes at the cost of lobotomizing the Dungeon and rendering it a docile vegetable, only able to respond when poked directly. The random encounter table, properly used, is an acceptable compromise that preserves both the integrity of the Dungeon and the wits of the Game Master.

What is true of the encounter is also true of treasure, disposition, and even weather - all tables that are not worth taking the time to make a conscious decision over. It is far more useful to turn one's creative energy toward integrating the results of those rolls into the world.

A GM who is attempting to create a Living Campaign must, for their own sanity, outsource the valuables of dungeons to a random treasure table lest they are seriously considering hand picking the contents of any number of unpredictable locales! Even in the cases where the treasure table has been overly generous, this is no strike against the practice of using such tools; overly generous results might mean that the room is heavily trapped and/or guarded by a powerful person/people/creature...it is best that in order to gain the wealth within, it will come at great personal risk.

Likewise, the random encounter table for a dungeon goes hand in hand with its disposition table. These are simple, easy to read, and quick to roll - it will not waste time in the session, if anything it will shave time down while simultaneously creating unforeseen situations where encounters are not automatically hostile and strange-but-fun roleplay options open up that would be difficult to replicate in a curated game.

Most random tables need not be rolled during a session, since the weather can be arbitrated with a dice roll and a journal note at any point in the lead-up to Game Day, for example.

While there is some respect to be had for the work ethic of the GM who would hand pick all the elements of their game, it is a matter of best practices that only the most useful aspects of said game be given attention so as to maximize their impact on the players...likewise, *overworking* on those aspects that hardly impact the players is a poor use of time/mental resources!

A monster can be killed but once; a coin pile is counted, collected, and then forgotten...of what use is it to pour over the rulebooks for the perfect combination of such and such equipment guarded by only so many monsters, carefully

tweaking and measuring every aspect of the actual act of adventuring? Truly, the concept of meticulous encounter balancing will go out the window at first contact with the Party anyway.
Dice are random, you cannot plan for a streak of good or bad luck!

Instead, use those hours to flesh out your town, create a new NPC, invent a new faction to introduce to the area...otherwise understood as: the parts of the game that players will continually engage in, that generate the majority of play. Pouring work into content that will generate more content is an investment of time and energy that will pay dividends by saving later time and energy - a burgeoning friendship with an NPC is an organic hook that only bears more fruit the more it is picked, for example.

Of course, interaction with the setting is made more potent with the application of a time standard...

NON-NEGOTIABLE: DEFINING THE PASSAGE OF TIME

Much has been made of the tracking of time within this work. This is necessary due to the heavy load that this one particular rule carries in a Living Campaign. The exclusion of consistent time tracking from contemporary tables has deactivated an easy mechanism that maximizes the number of players and Game Masters that can participate in an ongoing campaign; reintroducing 1:1 time likewise reactivates aspects and outcomes that have long been dismissed as non-viable or impossible by the broader hobby scene and is a core mechanical observance that is integral to creating a stable campaign that players return to over and over again.

As mentioned in THE PASSAGE OF TIME & EXPLORING THE DUNGEON (see pg.41), the utilization of 1:1 time allows for GMs to arbitrate all activities and answer questions posed by their players in the days between sessions. While off-the-cuff improvisational talent is admirable and useful within the context of Tabletop RPGs, explicitly creating a chronological space for individuals to think through their actions and potential consequences slows the game down to a manageable level for the new Game Master taking their first shaky steps toward beginning a campaign of their own.

The initial impression of many that first hear of this particular rule is that it is a recipe for over-complicated situations and causes an unworkable amount of session planning for the GM as they struggle to parse the incoming information. The skeptic may even dismiss the idea out of hand and proclaim it dubious that any table has ever implemented its game in this way, modern or otherwise.

This is not so!

The reality of 1:1 time is counterintuitive from the perspective of the contemporary GM - the truth is that implementation of out-of-session time passage MASSIVELY slows the rate at which the GM must process and arbitrate that information. The players' commands and pursuits trickle in a few at a time through phone call, text, or email whereby the GM can take their time and carefully consider the circumstances and rolls that must be made in order to satisfactorily make a decision on the outcome of the order.

Even allowing for the above to be an exaggeration and authorial bias, the question remains: what exactly is so much more difficult about tracking the passage of time that creating complex flow-chart screenplays serves as the more reasonable solution? Many dozens of hours of planning can go into a traditionally constructed session while actual potential play time is significantly lower.

The average GM will sit down for several hours per week usually planning in one of two ways:

1) They spend much of that time gaming out as many potential scenarios as possible, betting that they know the habits and desires of the players well enough that they will not find themselves in a situation entirely beyond what they have anticipated. Functionally it is a bet.
2) They spend that time crafting a narrative funnel that the players are expected to continue through. If they are talented, the players will be corralled along the story with sufficient motivation to willingly engage with the tracks of the railroad; if they are not talented, the players will become frustrated and attempt to break free of the chains clumsily placed upon them.

It is important to note about either method: both are divorced entirely from the ongoing input of the players and so the GM must provide both input and output, players exist to consume the output of the Game Master and are not permitted to input their creativity into the game beyond what occurs within a 3-5 hour period once a week (sometimes less). The GM that freezes time between sessions MUST be someone of exceptional talent with a group that possesses an unusual amount of patience and drive, otherwise the campaign falls apart. Stories permeate online forums and message boards of weekly campaigns that start strong, then begin to slow...a few people begin to grow tardy, then one session is conducted every other week, then one a month, then a hiatus, followed finally by death.

This is not to criticize those GMs and imply that they are UNTALENTED or somehow unworthy - it is unfair to demand that every person who runs a campaign must also be a talented writer, improv actor, and empath able to make snap narrative judgments that players will be consistently enthusiastic about. They must also be willing to work for hours without pay during the week and possess a work ethic that allows them to more easily recover between sessions, otherwise they will burn out. That the above outcome repeats ad infinitum across the breadth of the sum total of campaign tables with little deviation suggests that it might be a symptom of a common disease instigated by the received wisdom of the greater hobby community!

By shackling the table to a time standard, red meat is returned to the bones of a skeletal system; by having a concrete measurement of the passage of time that limits players to a single chronological space within the game they are paradoxically able to indulge in nearly any pursuit that they wish. Players can become INCREDIBLY active within the worlds of their adventure - through text, email, phonecall, and/or direct message - they will inform the GM in real time, as part of the game, what they desire to pursue and the manner in which they will pursue it. There is no longer a need for the infinite flow chart or the exhaustive performance of off-rails improvisational play; the GM will spend their time instead on engaging with their friends and bringing their world more and more to life.

But what if the players do not engage out-of-session with the described enthusiasm? This is to be expected at first...in my case, very little outside activity was logged when I first began to run the game in this style. Slowly, it became clear to the players that they had become truly free to do as they saw fit; a request to scout around a village yielded the location of the raiders that had been plaguing them for weeks. That player, excited, began to make more requests: could she get with the wizard Player Character to teleport back to the capital? Was it possible to organize a supplier of food to the starving villagers who had their stores raided in the middle of winter? Could she ask the shady black marketeers for help in tracking the location of a dragon spotted on the horizon of the village?

Another player saw this and asked to train volunteers in the ways of his barbarian, to help combat the raiders. Another designated the space between sessions as the time that he would brew his potions and write his scrolls. Another didn't feel like engaging outside the session much at all; she was content with the activity afforded to her at the time of play. All of this is fine - if none of the players engage with the downtime, bring in a monster, uncover a dungeon, introduce a new villain, and inform them of such things with a message! Being directly engaged will likely spur them to some action. If not, then it is probable that they are more casual players anyway...it is unlikely that long hours spent writing meticulous adventures would move them to engage enthusiastically either.

The players will plot among themselves and dabble in aspects of their characters they had not thought to use: one player realized that a spell existed that she could use to repair the damaged crops of the village...a rather mundane effect quite useless in the dungeon, but wildly useful when trying to help a beleaguered community!

Another repeated question I often hear on this subject is: "what if the player characters are still in a dungeon when the session ends?"

The structure of the game naturally directs players away from this situation. As downtime has become more valuable under the new gameplay architecture, GMs will find that players don't *want* to spend overlong in a hostile environment where they can't pursue their personal goals and submit meaningful downtime orders - camping in the dungeon, then, would be the most BORING option given the choices available to the players!

"What if they are trapped in a dungeon then?"

The vast majority of these games have a large number of tools, skills, spells, and abilities that are meant to aid player characters in various activities as they travel about the world. Perhaps a door closes and locks behind the player characters as they venture into a crypt...is the door too tough to break down? Do they not have spells that allow them to teleport out? Are they able to dig out from another location? Is there a switch or button that will reopen the door? Can the lock not be picked? And even then, as previously noted, certain events or goals like "escape" could be negotiated in the downtime, though not without risk.

It is true that allowing time to advance outside of the session creates an environment where the players are required to move quickly before their window of rapid activity closes. They will need to strategize with one another and move on their objectives purposefully to maximize the time spent in the session. They will need to leave behind old habits that prevent them from operating efficiently.

For example, combat is the most obvious part of the session that has the potential to drag the night down into a multi-hour slog if steps are not taken to manage the time it takes players to perform their character's actions. In any complex system, there are ways to trim the fat. An example of how I handle managing combat at my table is: players roll their attacks or cast their spells or activate their abilities, total their modifiers, and roll damage for the round - all together at the same time; the individual results of each player is recorded on a piece of scrap paper that is read off to the GM in the order of their initiative. Upon finding out the results of their recorded action, they immediately roll for the actions on their next turn and again record the results.

The above example is somewhat of a digression, but it serves to illustrate a point that assessing the viability of a new rule's mechanical implementation while using old methods of play that have been in use since BEFORE that rule's issuance is not a reason to disregard the new rule, but it may be a reason to alter the method of following that rule. As certain circumstances arise at the table, the players will naturally begin to alter their behavior as they attempt to find habits and methods that are further optimized for this new style of play: they will save non-necessary time-consuming activities for the end of session, or for downtime in most cases.

The recovery of downtime activity as a function of out-of-session play optimizes for the raison d'être of certain classes that are too often denied the full use of their greatest talents. The most obvious example of this restoration is in the primary function of any class of player character that requires stealth and cunning. The assassin, for example, is not often able to get out on their own to conduct their grisly work in typical play since the other PCs are not ALL going to possess the appropriate skills to assist in such endeavors. However, with 1:1 time the assassin could work their contracts in the space between sessions, where the necessary rolls are performed by the either Player or GM and the player is informed of their character's success or failure.

Rogues are meant to engage in thievery and heists, how often would such characters involve classes that do not possess the talents of a career thief? The planning stages and the heist itself might be conducted entirely via message, again between Player and GM. The character being arrested or finding themselves on the run would be quite the interesting quest to start in the next session!

Wizards are scholars of magic. Sure they are practitioners of the arcane arts, but they also are often talented craftsmen, enchanters, scribes, and researchers. Out-of-session is the perfect time for such characters to investigate the mysteries that so often intrigue members of their class!

There are a number of second-order effects observed from the implementation of 1:1 time, such as the growth of the number of player characters each player has access to. Player characters will occasionally take on activities that, when enough days are needed, the character will still be indisposed by the time of the following session. The creation of a new low-level character occurs at this stage; sometimes this is an individual from a background, sometimes this is a henchman that a player has taken a liking to - often it is simply a class that a player wants to try.

A stable of alternate PCs has significantly alleviated the preoccupation with character death at the table, since each player can have several PCs they care about, the sting of a favorite's death hurts less. Usually these lower level alternates will have some connection to each other - everyone has **someone** who would go the distance to resurrect them!

When a majority of players can't make it to the session due to real life scheduling conflicts, the session can continue as the players that CAN make it may decide to adventure with their lower level characters rather than canceling the session. The individuals who can't be present do not miss the action on their primary character and those who do show up, get to run a lower stakes session where they can learn about the function of other classes while exploring a new dungeon in search of loot and monsters!

And speaking of the Dungeon...

CODIFYING THE DUNGEON CRAWL

What is true of time tracking in the Campaign as a whole is also true of the Dungeon in particular. Time matters in a dungeon and it will need to be wielded by the GM to establish a coherent experience at their table. The grinding oppression of exploring a dangerous ruin filled with traps and monsters of all sorts requires a standard; the passing of time imposes clear constraints on player movement. Noisy activity potentially brings monstrous attention to the interlopers who seek to take the glittering gold held within. The usage of turns will clearly demarcate player activity and monster activity: indicating to the GM when it is appropriate to roll on the random encounter table that has been prepared for the dungeon area.

The ruleset chosen by the GM will have in-built methods for determining things like spell duration, food rationing, equipment weight, and the discovery of sneaking characters - these circumstances are still very much a part of the ongoing tradition of tabletop RPGs. It's likely that the GM will need to make some judgment calls to adjudicate dubious player application of their chosen rulebook, this is a necessary skill regardless of whether the GM decides that they will apply the advice written here or not. There is always an edge case to be had and a referee does need to rule one way or another.

Imposing coherent, turn-based movement linked to the passing of time (as described in THE PASSAGE OF TIME & EXPLORING THE DUNGEON; see pg.41) upon the campaign is a completion of the core loop long ago set down within the first RPG rulebooks:

the Dungeon is built into the bones of the mechanics and this lineage has not yet passed from various editions and other independent titles. A certain skepticism is to be expected on the part of the players - they are creatures of habit and will be unsure of leaving behind the methods they hold to be tried and true.

If they are patient and willing to at least give it a shot, they will be pleasantly surprised as the turn-order structure demands constant engagement from every player present.

For example:
Devyn the Fighter has sharp eyes to go with his sharp sword, he'll need to pay attention to look for traps and incoming monsters.
Bollin the Thief is a talented lockpick, he'll need to work on getting the doors that he can work open.
Mog the Barbarian is big and tough, he'll need to have his axe ready as he warily peers into the darkness, ready to swing on anyone or anything that takes a hostile step toward the party.
Vitelexia the Sorceress casts spells of light to illuminate her fellows' path. She makes sure to stay behind Mog.

The use of a Party Caller will greatly reduce the real world time it takes to move individual PCs down a dungeon hallway, as they will functionally be the party leader - moving people together and informing the GM of any actions taken in their allotted time. This player will likely slip into a role where they draw conversation out of the others on behalf of the GM; further, the other players will willingly pay attention after they've handed control of their character to someone else...what if they want to break away to check something out? They need to stay focused so as not to miss anything!

Additionally, when the GM is consulting their encounter tables or the dungeon map, they can rely on the Caller to corral their fellows and push them forward. Simply asking who wants to do the job is usually enough to draw out latent leadership tendencies and all the GM should do is gently remind any dissenters that their characters will be free to break away if they seriously disagree with a Caller's decision-making.

Functionally, nothing has changed about what the players actually do around the table: they still move their miniatures down corridors, they still stop to discuss, they still roll their dice, but now they do these things within a structure that allows for the Dungeon to respond. They feel the weight of plumbing the depths of a place that hates them. At the end of their portion of the Dungeon Turn, they will wait with anticipation for the GM to roll on the encounter table to see if something wanders their way, they will wonder while looking: "will I notice something sneaking up on us?" or "will we run into something hostile?". The tension only grows as abilities are spent and injuries are accrued.

At my table it is always a fun moment when the PCs have moved as far as they can in their allotted time and the Caller confirms that they've expended all possible actions for that turn...because looking them in the eyes and saying as ominously as possible, "Now it's the Dungeon's turn" never fails to make players feel at least a little more tense.

It's simple enough to mark the passing time in the GM's notes with each instance you hear "we're done with our turn". Eventually, one way or another, they will need to leave the dungeon and the GM will be able to inform them how much time has passed since their descent into the earth. It is a small detail, but not an unimportant one: something can stir in a player when they can feel the march of time within a campaign.

FOR EVERY PLAYER, A MULTITUDE

The commonly accepted method of character creation is akin to creating a starring role in a television series. This character is usually created with the intention of engaging with a full story arc, culminating in a satisfying conclusion, and will be the primary vehicle for the player to engage with the world. They are the heroes of the story, the plot revolves around their pursuit of some larger objective and weaves their individual backstories concretely into the overarching narrative created by the GM.

The primary flaw of such an experience is the singular nature of the heroes coupled with the need for random dice rolls in order for that character to not die. The GM is presented with an unsolvable dilemma: they are expected to create fun and balanced encounters that must also be unlikely to be lethal...while at the same time completely fooling the players into believing in the terrible danger of the whole scenario. While the lack of lethality is never explicitly stated as an expectation in most media, it is implied by the assumption in source material that each player will have but a single character: in the event of character death, a dead PC is likely the only one that the player has immediately at their disposal. It can make for quite an awkward evening if someone is removed from the game halfway through.

Some tables circumvent this issue by informing players to have back ups prepared in the event of PC death. While this does work, it is imperfect; players feel no connection to these sudden additions to the party and their integration is often clunky to implement. Occasionally this alternate only stays with the party long enough to resurrect the player's initial character after which they simply leave the game until such a time that they are needed again; this method is at its most effective at the very beginning of a campaign when none of the characters are well known to their players yet and the attachment to a particular PC hasn't quite taken root - in fact, I recommend a player to have an alternate PC or two for the first few sessions of my own game! The lowest level PCs are unlikely to have alternate characters naturally introduced before they've gotten their first real taste of money and power...hard to hire henchmen while broke, after all.

It is a fact that many contemporary rulesets go to great lengths to try and prevent character death with the inclusion of all sorts of mechanics that offer opportunities for the character to stabilize their condition. This expectation is a source of many heartaches within the hobby as new GMs and new players unexpectedly find themselves in the above described position without the working knowledge required to quickly fix it. When the unusual failure happens, it is not uncommon for tempers to flare as the death of a PC could spell the end of an evening for a player - no fun for them! It's possible that mechanics designed to alleviate this problem instead can make it explosive for the minority of situations where the death of a Player Character *does* occur.

The suggested solution then builds from the instruction to create multiple PCs: assume that player characters will naturally take on associates, followers, hirelings, henchmen, or otherwise attach themselves to an organization - whether they found the organization or swear loyalty to it is irrelevant. Eventually a plurality of problems will manifest and the PCs will find themselves in a position where they may need to be in multiple places at once. This is when the player would take on a second character, created at the lowest level or drawn from a trusted henchman, and send them off to handle those issues that the initial party can't be present to defeat. Another example is how a character would be created if the initial PC is stuck in the process of leveling up. All of these characters built in such a way will have the investment of the player who created them since they will have the time to grow attached. A network of interconnected player characters will organically develop, enriching the milieu and giving the players incredible amounts of influence over the creative direction of the Campaign, all while encouraging them to perform within the mindset of their accrued personas.

Outside of this passive collection of PCs, the application of Training Time and Training Costs in order for them to gain the next level creates a situation where the player character can't, under any circumstances, pause training to continue on an adventure or downtime activity without forfeiting the costs and time that they have already paid. A player that finds their PC still occupied with training by the time of the in-person game can be encouraged to create an alternate character for themselves. The accrual of power that confounds many a GM can be mitigated if the offending PCs are indisposed and low-level alternates are needed to be employed. This gives the Game Master time to acclimate to the evolving circumstances around PC abilities and skills.

Having multiple player characters per player solves for many problems with dangerous combat. The death of a PC will likely still be a source of frustration, but it no longer ejects the player from the game or forces them to play something unfamiliar/unexpected that they have no love for, built only in response to character death. The player will be able to call on the various associates of their fallen PC and play with their alternates; these could work to resurrect their fallen comrade or the player might decide to shift full-time into the back up. The tightrope walk of encounter balance is no longer the force it once was when the game is not required to come to a grinding halt in the event that the monsters roll particularly well that evening.

While it is my opinion that the primary advantage of multiple PCs is the mitigation of player death anxiety, there is another advantage to be had that must be expressed to provide a more complete picture: the accrual of a stable of PCs provides a breadth of potential experiences and does not shackle a player to the workings and mind of a single individual. Playing with the same tool over and over again is fine for many, but for many more the novelty wears off and they begin to wonder what it might be like to play something else...or more seriously, they may grow bored with the Campaign as a whole. In a Living Campaign, a single player may find themselves taking on the roles of villains, heroes, anti-heroes, and/or anti-villains! There is nothing beyond their reach!

With all the ways PCs might otherwise become occupied, even the lowest level addition to a player's repertoire is unlikely to stay at the bottom rung forever; in my Campaign, some player's henchmen ended up surpassing their employers in both wealth and experience!

THE SKILL LIST AS A "NON-GAME"

As previously mentioned, the skill list is a nearly universal mechanic implemented in almost every rules system that currently exists. There is a sense that in order to be taken seriously as an RPG, said RPG must contain some sort of measure of the skills and expertise of the player characters and/or non-player characters. How else are the players supposed to figure out what their characters are able to do?

There is a fundamental misapplication in the current-day method of using skill lists in the largest games of this type: the characters are not supposed to be competent in a very small handful of abilities (and subsequently incompetent with all the others) and they almost certainly are not supposed to be used consistently over relatively mundane tasks. There exists a proper usage of such rules that allows skills to become useful tools for quickly arbitrating the results of the myriad actions the players might wish to take with their PCs. There also exists an *improper* usage that is a sort of randomized non-game that can exist within the overall design of a system.

"Proper" usage then would be similar to the following: the GM may find themselves in a situation with an antagonistic NPC where said NPC has several options they wish to take. For this example, let's say a bandit lord is attempting to violently attack the PCs and take their valuables: now if the battle begins to turn against the bandit, the GM may find themselves unsure of what to do. Would this bandit commit to the assault, intent on recovering something for the bloody effort? Or would he pull back so as not to lose more men to enemies with more bite than the usual marks?

The GM can arbitrarily assess the likelihood of the options, assign a ballpark percentage value, and then roll to see which choice the bandit makes. In other words, the GM has outsourced the decision to the dice in order to save their mental horsepower for other challenges. The idea of the "skill list", properly applied, will function in much the same way. The player characters are highly competent individuals, they will be able to do a great number of things should they decide to do them. The value in the skill list comes in those situations where the result isn't necessarily obvious. An example would be reading a map and knowing which road to take; such a thing would not require a skill check from anyone, asking for one in this situation is a superfluous roll with characteristics more related to dice gambling than a Role Playing Game. A way to fill time and roll dice with no consistent logic.

An opposite example: the table might go off-road at some point for any number of reasons; if they walk for a long time without clear markers of where to go, it would be appropriate to make a skill check of some kind in order to arbitrate the question "did the player characters get lost?". In the old days of the hobby, the procedure for the above was discerned through random application while the party adventures in unexplored wilderness. It is specifically noted that such procedures were NOT needed when the party possessed a correct map and followed it.

This is the logic that informs the application of the skill list.

The skill list is an added layer to this acceptable randomness; is every party equally likely to become lost in the wilderness? Would more nature oriented characters not be more adept at navigating unexplored terrain of a type they are comfortable in?

The only question that should be asked whenever the GM requires a roll for the use of a skill is "how difficult will this be to accomplish?", if the answer to that question is either "it's easy" or "it's impossible" the roll ought not be required. There are many cases where a GM will ask for a roll that they believe will be impossible to make, only for the player to roll a 20 on the die. If the GM denies the success then what was the point of the roll? If they allow a success for an absurdity, what is the point of logical constraint? The Campaign's internal logic is damaged when these things are allowed to happen; the Campaign is enervated as the players increasingly become unable to suspend their disbelief.

The compulsion to allow for impossible rolls is born out of a desire to placate insistent players (or more charitably, to be accommodating to friends). The GM allows a player to roll for the impossible so that they can feel like they still have some measure of control, but the reality is they were supposed to fail. This will work 95% of the time, as you will always be able to say "maybe if you rolled a 20".

5% of the time is when they roll that 20 and a minor immersion disruption occurs. That 5% can cascade as the Campaign continues, growing into a major immersion disruption for the players if rolls are always allowed.

The opposite compulsion exists for easy rolls, though the intent is related: The GM is under the mistaken impression that rolling for something every couple of minutes means that the game is being played. A great many slapstick routines would look like a series of rolled 1's where people break their wrists opening doors or catastrophically slip on puddles. This can turn into a tremendous frustration for players. It is an annoyance to roll for standard things that any commoner would be able to accomplish. This mentality creates a situation where the player characters feel disrespected by the very game they participate in!

If the advice to begin play at the lowest level of experience is taken - then the relatively weak PCs will still NEED to be afforded a respect by the GM's rulings: checking a PC's dexterity if they try to cut an apple is the same as calling them children. It is (probably unintentional) mockery.

It is a far more consistent experience to allow the players to perform their actions as they see fit, with a skill roll called for only in those situations where the result is not obvious to the GM. There may be grumblings in those instances where a skill check is deemed impossible...though the players are not likely to complain when they are assumed competent in the results of their orders. In the end, maintaining control over the internal consistency of the game will be a good thing for the overall viability and long-term health of the Campaign.

THE DUNGEON AS A LIVING ENTITY

The Dungeon, as it is currently conceived of in the broader hobby, appears to be a vestigial organ; it is attached to nearly every campaign in some capacity, though it has very little supporting its use across the various rules platforms. The current-day dungeon is a curated experience, like a ride at an amusement park, where the players enter, proceed through different rooms and floors, occasionally acquire treasure, and then eventually fight a powerful creature or character at the end before exiting. It is not considered strictly necessary to the greater campaign, and could be considered detrimental if one takes into account the writing hours that are required to create such an experience relative to the payoff that players get out of it.

The Dungeon as a concept is carried across years, across editions, across systems...yet its place in the hobby is treated almost as a rote nuisance.

The problem with the Modern Dungeon is a two prong issue:
1) Each of them are *mechanically* complex. Dungeons require time to conceive, map, and fill with monsters, traps, and gear. They exist to tell a story and so must be woven into the "Grand Narrative". Its content must be narratively related to the plot points the players are aware of, otherwise why would anyone even go there?
2) They are *conceptually* simple. They are used **once** and they have no potential future function after their narrative utility has been spent. The only reason they exist is because the Story demands it - and it shows.

The values have been inverted with regard to the Dungeon, many aspects are improved at the level of ACTUAL PLAY when the above values are restored to their original understanding:
1) They ought to be mechanically simple. The vast majority of dungeons only need to be several rooms linked by passages and hallways (maybe a secret passage or two thrown in) with a few descriptors chosen for the sake of being able to paint a picture. The particulars of their design should be done quickly: treasure placement ought to be outsourced to random tables, inhabitants could be chosen similarly with random tables, traps placed near treasure, doors, or otherwise where it feels right. They can exist as self-contained adventure locations and *do not* need to be grafted onto some larger narrative.
2) They should be conceptually complex. The Dungeon serves as the primary method that adventurers become stronger and acquire the wealth that allows them to mark the world. The dungeons exist because they are a part of the setting, whether or not they make sense in the context of some narrative is irrelevant. Perhaps after they are cleared, the player characters will choose to live there! Or will the cleared dungeon left idle long enough attract new inhabitants? The potentialities spill out - this place could be *anything* in a month or two!

A GM's faculties should be turned toward making the process of creation easier for themselves through random generation. Turning the decision-making around a dungeon's design into an external process will free the GM to fill their milieu with the various elements of the player character's backgrounds, as well as allow them the time to reflect on the changes the players will begin to make in the setting as they enrich the world with their characters' decisions. One way or another, the players will be traversing the world that the GM lays out for them - what functional difference does it make then if they do it as part of a story arc or if they do it by their own choice?

There is no real difference!

There are criticisms that say that these disconnected dungeons will help create a sense of listlessness within the Campaign, like the players are lurching from ruin to ruin without any sort of driving motivation. Such things are purely a matter of execution on the part of the GM: the professionally minded Game Master will observe the results of a dungeon they have generated and work backwards to let it help inform the setting. They will ask themselves what the people in the area (if any) think of the known points of interest around their community. The professional GM, in the event of listless players, might ask about the progress on the player characters' backgrounds - have they been thinking about using their wealth to do the things they *really* want to do?

Additionally, the Dungeon is not always required to be an underground ruin or a cave network. A "Dungeon" is any concept that follows the above baseline criteria (linked areas, secrets, traps, treasure, inhabitants) - it is perfectly acceptable for a city block to be a dungeon, or a particularly dense forest. A variety of interesting locations could be used as a place for the party to explore, smash, and loot for their own personal gain.

The Dungeon is the lynchpin that holds the entire core gameplay loop of many rules systems together: it is the primary economic driver of the low-to-mid level adventurer and an easy source of conflict to turn a party of strangers into fire-forged friends. From the humble beginnings of a character's career focused primarily on the pursuit of the Dungeon (and the wealth contained therein), the game will grow in scale as low level characters become high level characters and they begin to establish permanent marks upon the places they choose to reside through the acquisition of noble titles, the purchase of land, the construction of a stronghold. It is best practice then, for there to always be a dungeon available to new characters to cut their teeth on, so that the players will be able to raise up alternate PCs or strengthen followers for more adventures with higher stakes and requiring the aid of many to help.

Individual player characters will eventually transcend the **need** for the Dungeon when they grow strong enough, but the players themselves will always have at least one foot in the dungeon/loot/level cycle through their other, low-to-mid level adventurers. What keeps this loop from growing stale if its design concept will not be changing between adventures?

It is the idea that the players themselves will determine which dungeons warrant an expedition and put up the coin that will pay their underlings to go out and conquer whichever evil hole needs to be conquered. Intent does much to affect perception in this regard!

If the GM is funneling the players from dungeon to dungeon in the form of a linear schema, then of course the game *will* grow stale. A key aspect is the players being able to answer the question "why is my character here?" without hesitation or strain, which should be adequately clear to them at all times:

"because they chose to be" - this is the abstracted answer that covers all potential scenarios of worth from the perspective of the players.

ORGANICALLY GROWN ADVENTURES

The linear campaign model is static in its implementation, requiring a great deal of behind-the-scenes work on the part of GM to sufficiently convince the players that they are affecting change in the setting. A Living Campaign creates conditions that allow content to spontaneously manifest independent of the Game Master's input; player orders have a compounding effect that steadily increases the complexity of the Campaign *organically*. On the other side of this, the common mental mode of many Game Masters is that their craft exists somewhere between scripting a television show and writing a book; much of the advice that currently exists are cautionary warnings to not deviate too far into this mentality, where the GM is advised to maintain a vague "balance" of scripted events vs. player choice.

While it is *understandable* that a contemporary might have these reactions, it is not an excuse to reject the contents contained in the words herein. My sympathies end at "understanding" and do not progress further.

The commonly accepted methods of constructing adventures involves establishing a larger outline of a story, with a primary villain and/or organization with a goal that may or may not come to fruition as the story progresses. Once this overarching plot is charted the GM goes about the task of integrating player backstories into their larger narrative, making only small alterations here and there to the finer details so that the player driven side stories line up parallel with the GM's primary plotline. Hooks to various stages of each adventure must be placed periodically, the candy of the early adventures slowly leading further up the narrative chain where final resolution comes as the final encounter with the main antagonist approaches. After this, the Campaign ends and play stops for a time.

Player choice in this scenario comes in the form of roleplay, where they might be able to give a rousing speech or make a choice affecting the outcome of one or more NPCs; they have very little actual control over how the scenario comes to fruition or the environment beyond what is immediately in front of them. It is true that this is usually perfectly fine from the perspective of the players (at first): a hook well-baited certainly feels like a choice, but in reality is the imposition of a storyline structure that the players must adhere to and is successfully pulled off inconsistently over a long period of time. Simply put: this style is *extremely difficult* to replicate across GMs, across campaigns and is largely a matter of practiced *talent and personal interest.*

Another problem that is brought on by the modern method described is the enormous amount of work relative to player engagement. The number of writing hours that goes into producing between four to six concurrent, personal storylines that all run parallel to a larger narrative that hinges on the player's willingness to play along with the hooks presented is an incredible undertaking for the GM-Aspirant. A player either chooses to take the bait or their portion is lost until the next opportunity to wiggle the lure in front of them. It is not uncommon for players to take the hook only because they feel it is vaguely rude NOT to if their Game Master's enthusiasm gives away how much of the session perhaps hangs on their seizing of what dangles before them..

A Living Campaign functions differently - it mechanically encourages player engagement: as in, it is driven by what the players themselves would like to do.

Adventures are actively sought out (or encountered) and taken on by the players as their characters traverse the world. With time progressing in 1:1, they are free to pursue their interests, engage in their class functions, or otherwise prepare for adventure - while the GM is given real-life time to decide the details of the avenues the players have decided to go down. Isn't knowing the direction of a party of PCs several days in advance better than having to try and guess their reactions to cultivated scenarios conceived of with only the most minimal levels of their input?

Inter-session correspondence has the effect of getting the players to write the Game Master's notes FOR them...and they will thank the GM for the privilege! The exhaustive planning needs of the Grand Narrative are abandoned in favor of enriching the milieu: setting up factions, creating major personalities in the region, populating the countryside with dungeons, etc. The backgrounds of the player characters will inform the starting area and help fill out the cast of NPCs. The factions will be the new drivers of continuing the adventure; establishing a handful of such factions in the area and then releasing them against one another and the party is all the motivation the players will need to go forward.

An example from my table is the adventures within a village hex: The PCs had been contracted to retrieve a magic lamp for a wealthy patron. The lamp, however, is located within the hoard of a dragon, deep in the local mountain range. Additionally, the area has an orc warband that has cut the village off from commerce and trade, as well as a Thieves Guild black market with elite bugbear bodyguards who have decided to take advantage of the chaos.

None of the individual pieces of the above scenario is particularly strange or complex. The setting has an orc problem in the countryside and opportunistic humans took it upon themselves to make a quick buck. Being so close to the mountains was a good opportunity to add a powerful monster...and a flying monster is particularly terrifying in untamed wilderness, so a dragon was appropriate. I have used encounter tables of my own design to determine which factions might be located in a region when I am unsure or uninspired.

The characters themselves had their own memorable and defining character moments:

The Druid learned how powerful she could be when she led orc raiding parties into the forest.

The Barbarian, being a half-orc, decided he had something to prove and challenged the chieftain in a ritual duel.

The Fighter/Sorcerer was sent to defend the town by his patron and had grown attached to the townsfolk and, inspired by their determination, petitioned his own patron to send relief forces.

There were several more with the rest of the party, but the point has been made.

All of these things were willingly chosen by the players and pursued during out-of-session play. Characters investigated the area, tailing enemy scouts when they saw them; increasingly hostile messages were sent to antagonistic NPCs, and they alleviated the problems of allied NPCs. The orc chieftain once hired an assassin to kill a character friendly to the players merely to deliver a note that he accepted the challenge to a duel, a result adjudicated in the middle of the week with the roll of a percentage dice.

This is not to say that the likes of a Great Villain, or Big Bad Evil Guy (BBEG) will never be seen again, quite the contrary, the players will simply tell you who they hate the most. They will engage negatively with this NPC, who will then be forced to engage negatively with them - perhaps the antagonist will grow stronger as the two sides wage an escalating struggle for survival. Establishing majorly high level actors out in the world will serve in this regard as well: these figures, or associates of these figures, can find their attention drawn to the rising power of the player characters, setting off a conflict of the ages!

The Organic Adventure is not a list of don'ts for the prospective GM - it is a call to allow the players to fully assume control of their own actions and turn the referee's creative powers upon the aspect of the game that they are sure to enjoy: the world that they built.

A series of these adventures, spontaneously generated by the players themselves, will award much loot and reward: money, equipment, land, etc. These rewards will provide the capital that will allow the growth of a character's power and influence both mechanically with experience awards and narratively with command of castles and soldiers. They can achieve none of these things without continually going out to find it!

TO THE VICTOR, THE SPOILS

The common perception of encumbrance is that it is a nuisance to track and not fun for the GM to enforce. The suggestion that even coins ought to be included in this is simply beyond the pale for most!

If time tracking is the factor that binds players to their characters' perceptions in the world of the Campaign, then encumbrance is what forces the players to actually *live* there. Some amount of front-end preparatory work ought to be undertaken by the GM-Aspirant when they begin play in this manner: they should have any relevant charts for determining how much weight can be carried and also what items and equipment weigh - if no such chart exists in a convenient form, then perhaps the creation of a cheat sheet is necessary. A certain initial respect for a ruleset should be internalized by the GM; they should make serious attempts to follow the rules where applicable and consider whether their frustration is borne from the rules themselves or the GM's sub-optimal implementation of those rules.
It is not acceptable to give up before even trying to comply!

This is the space that encumbrance occupies: it is easy to include the encumbrance rules badly, but if the GM takes the time to adjust their habits and help their players adjust in turn, they will see that new interesting avenues of play are opened.

First, player choice with regard to the attributes of their characters are given more impact. For example, if the player decides to have low strength in order to have a more dexterous, mechanically deadly character, then they will be sacrificing potential gain in the form of treasure that they can carry for themselves and their fellows. If the seizing of loot is how experience is awarded, then leaving gold and items is a penalty on the level growth of the character.

Another example: if the player instead rejects charisma, then they may find that their character is poorly treated by the people and creatures they encounter due to low reaction rolls - quite the predicament while loaded down with valuable loot!

Second, the players will have a new aspect to consider when they venture out into the wilds in search of ruins and treasure. They will fill their packs with potions, food, and kits - only to realize that they don't have enough room for the coin that brought them out in the first place! A discussion will ensue about what to keep and what to leave. It is frustrating, but it is also *real* and it is an issue to be solved by the players themselves with manifold solutions to this relatively simple problem! To be in the middle of a hostile dungeon weighed down by loot and gold coins creates an atmosphere, a tension, that the players are sure to remember and look back on fondly (doubly so if they survive the ordeal). Remember: it is a tightrope walk between conducting a campaign that is too easy (creating boredom) and a campaign that revels in the unfair slaughter of player characters (creating frustration). Discarding tools that reliably aid in the maintenance of this balance is not to the ultimate benefit of the Campaign.

Which leads to a third point of interest: solutions lie in interaction with the Campaign and the players' commitment to playing the role of their characters.

Low level characters do have options early on in the Campaign - they could try to procure a wagon (or like transport), make attempts to hide their abandoned spoils until their return, or hire NPC villagers/hirelings to carry their belongings. The hireling has been the go-to method of transporting treasure at my table; the players have enjoyed growing attached to the randoms that sign up for their expeditions - they commonly demand that I provide a name on the spot (luckily several are kept written on a notecard, just in case!). A few of these hirelings have gone on to become followers of the PCs (or PCs themselves) and have struck out to become experienced adventurers!

Now, the inclusion of coins in the arithmetic of character encumbrance has raised the hackles of many fellow hobbyists who have heard the suggestion. There is a misunderstanding in the mind of those who hear this: they perceive the coin-weight to be primarily motivated by the pursuit of a misguided "realism"; a pursuit that is pointless when it is given primacy.
No, we are after something else entirely!
The primary effect of insisting that players weigh their coins is that they are introduced to a brand new problem: they must have somewhere to put the coins upon escaping the dungeon! A common negative phenomenon within the hobby is colloquially known as the "Murder-Hobo", PCs without any sort of ties or roots who wander from quest to quest killing, looting, selling, and then killing and looting some more. They always remain detached from the campaign milieu, never quite leaving the mentality of it being a game. Occasionally, this loop is applied to the peaceful villagers of the setting! Horror!

As with many of the common issues at tables, the murder-hobo is an epiphenomenon of the removal of certain mechanical disincentives. A major deterrent, I posit, against this behavior is encumbrance for coins; eventually, the player characters are REQUIRED to have some place to safely store their adventuring gains or else be permanently weighed down under their backpacks. They will need to involve themselves in a community and will need to play nice with that community if the players don't want their wealth seized by angry neighbors and used to hire assassins while their characters are out on an adventure!

Allowing coins to be weightless is, in effect, subsidizing rootless PCs and creating the conditions for wanton looting and slaughter by the players...and the rule governing subsidies is that one gets more of whatever is subsidized and less of whatever is restricted. Even if players are hellbent on never positively interacting with the milieu they will benefit from solving this problem; the creation of an off-the-grid compound hostile to all civilized peoples still roots them in the world and will be a source of great fun for the GM and the Players too!

Encumbrance is a load carrying pillar of a Living Campaign, hand waving away the rule that establishes a powerful motivation to construct or purchase permanent structures for long-term use and item storage is a significant factor in the creation of the rootless, marauding terrors that the PCs often become if you ask certain other tables.

THROUGH EXPERIENCE, STUDY, & GREAT EFFORT

A popular method for determining the gaining of character levels is by Checkpoint Leveling - the GM will award levels to all player characters in the party after an arbitrary number of sessions, combat scenarios, or story milestones. Absent players will usually be awarded as well, since it would be a problem for the GM's planned encounters if party members were not balanced with regard to one another. The benefits, such as they are, are focused on a reduction in "bookkeeping" required on the part of the players and/or the GM. It is simply easier to announce that the players have gained a level and message absent table members to level up before they come back to the next session.

There are a number of unfortunate second order effects exacerbated by the above method:
First, the arbitrary determination of character leveling detaches the player from the world. In this sense, the growing power and strength of a player character has almost nothing to do with growing wealth, influence, and class expertise; it is a decision made entirely on the whim of the GM...and whimsical decisions do much to reveal the person behind the proverbial curtain. Every time a GM cuts one of the mechanical straps that tethers characters to the Campaign, eventually it must be asked: what incentive is there for the players to remain suspended in their disbelief? This is not in the pursuit of some sense of "realism", it is a binding in the incentive structure that maintains the players' immersion in the world. Why should a player pay attention or care about anything in the game if

they are sure that merely being alive for certain milestones in a larger story arc will be rewarded with character levels?

Second, the rewarding of absent players subsidizes player tardiness; when a GM subsidizes absences they will be rewarded with more absences. Another common defense of Checkpoint Leveling is that withholding levels from absentee players could be considered punishing them in the case of certain real-life events. This is simply not the case - lack of reward is a NEUTRAL outcome. A punishment would be the REMOVAL of experience for certain out-of-game behaviors or actions. Experience for the collection of loot is a safeguard against unnecessary temporary absences and is unlikely to slow down any member of the party provided even semi-regular attendance...since players can allocate treasure shares, and thus a significant number of experience points, as they see fit. Players who missed a session or two can catch up in no time if their fellows agree to allocate them a larger share. A table that has cultivated a strong team dynamic will not balk at such things - except perhaps a player who plays a greedy thief...then some in-character, interparty negotiation is in order!

If the GM were to follow the instructional portion in ADVENTURES BOTH GRAND AND SMALL & THE LIVING DUNGEON (refer to pg. 31), they will have a variety of dungeons of varying strengths available to the party. In this case, the GM will be spending a significantly smaller amount of time balancing all combat to the current level of the PCs and more time creating dungeon scenarios and balancing the encounters within the context of those scenarios.

For example: a dungeon determined to be level 8 will have treasure, traps, loot, and monsters appropriate for a party of level 8 adventurers. Characters of 6th to 7th level might be able to tackle it, while levels 5 and lower will likely be met with disaster if they insist on plumbing its depths. Likewise a party of level 9 to 20 should have little trouble clearing it of its inhabitants and loot (and perhaps should have reduced experience rewards for the clearing of such a dungeon by an overleveled party).

This is to say, asymmetric leveling will be significantly less of an issue if the encounters are based on location and circumstance rather than a series of escalating, scripted events. High level characters can bring along their lower level fellows to let them get some serious on-the-job training!

Third, of the processes that could be made more efficient and the implementations that could be streamlined, it makes little sense to cut out entirely the numerical representation of the PCs' hard work. The gaining of experience is often done to the satisfaction of the players around the table - a simple resource that as they watch grow, they anticipate the day that they can level their characters and grow stronger. Additionally, the claim that checkpoint leveling speeds things up or is simpler to implement does not survive contact with reality: it is common to see characters awarded levels in the middle of the session, where the game stops for the players to quickly level them up, which can be a complicated endeavor in several rulesets. Sometimes they don't see this award coming and must learn the next level's abilities that have become available - doing this to new players trying to learn a complicated game is almost cruel!

But it is not enough to tear down common practices though, something must be built in its place:

Awarding experience for the securing of valuables should be tied to a common monetary unit of value - in the case of my table, this is the gold coin. By placing experience value on the securing of gold and equipment, the arithmetic of the players is altered regarding how they assess scenarios that manifest at the table. Whereas before they might attack all that come their way, now they find themselves in a situation where they are loaded down with gold and items - they need to escape before they are overwhelmed by their opponents.

Tying all experience point awards to violence is a subsidy on violence! Likewise, including other avenues of gaining strength is a dilution of the value of violent solutions to encountered scenarios. Other incentivized choices create a richer experience for both GM and Player as the murder-hobo subsidies are slowly removed from the mental scale within the players' heads.

An alternative criteria to mitigate these tendencies is the awarding of experience based on GM discretion with regard to the roleplay performance of the players in the game.

While this is a step in the right direction, it is a suboptimal solution in that it does not provide adequate motivation for the pursuit of adventure and treasure since it relies wholly on the arbitrary awarding of experience. We, as human beings, are often blind to our own patterns; in games at this level of mechanical complexity, it is usually best not to over-rely on one's own judgment for all cases.

Perhaps there are some GMs who will be able to conduct their game in this way while consistently awarding experience for good roleplaying, but it is unlikely to be the best practice for a majority of tables as evidenced by this alternative method being well considered in the broader contemporary hobby but almost entirely unused.

Tying experience growth to monetary value creates a consistent system that rewards adventuring, teamwork, and roleplay (what is negotiation with a Quest Giver NPC for better rewards if not roleplay?) while also helping to disincentivize bloodbaths.

Next, a character that reaches the threshold for the next level should not be able to instantaneously rise to the next level. Capping XP rewards at the threshold for the next character level is a preventative measure that heavily discourages that player from attempting to level their character in the middle of the session, forcing the game to stop until they are ready. It firmly places character leveling into the realm of downtime between sessions, where time continues to progress at 1:1.

If complaints are raised on this front, it would do the players well to be gently reminded that there will be plenty of experience points to be had in the form of future gold and combat encounters and that they should not fret that their character is indisposed with the training required to reach their new level.

If a PC has enough experience to grow in level, then they will need a trainer if they are below a certain amount of expertise. This is a great opportunity to introduce a new character who will serve as yet another node in the patronage network of NPCs that help enrich the lives (and opportunities) of the party. These mentor NPCs will require gold before they take on the task of training a PC to the next level...if the PC is lacking in funds perhaps they might owe their mentor a favor to be cashed at a later date.

If the PC is above a certain level of expertise, they will be able to become a trainer themselves: receiving their dues from their mentees in addition to no longer requiring a trainer of their own.

This evolution is representative of their achievement of a personal proficiency that allows them to perform adequate self-study to grow stronger. Nearly every aspect of the game can be turned around to the *overall* benefit of the players, even if a character takes some short-term loss for the time being - it is important to conceptualize it as making the Campaign stronger, as the loss teaches the players a lesson. In its own way, the Campaign is akin to a hunted deer: isn't it wasteful to throw out any parts of the animal that might be used to the hunter's benefit? Every part of the deer ought to be utilized and benefit the hunter and the hunter's family.

It will likewise be to the benefit of the table if the GM takes the time to first understand what exactly is lost when certain rules are thrown out.

As the GM-Aspirant accrues working knowledge of the rules they play with, they'll achieve proficiency - with proficiency they will be able to handle the increasingly complex adjudications required of them as their players get more comfortable in the setting and their creativity can be funded with loot secured from adventure.

Campaigns develop over time and so do GMs to meet the needs of these campaigns...

CAMPAIGNS GROW LIKE A MUSCLE

The Game Master who takes the time to create a campaign should treat themselves kindly in this task, as the building of a vibrant setting does not happen in a single day. The method prescribed in the instructional portion of the previous section attempts to reasonably chart the beginning stages of the Campaign for the prospective GM and provide them a basic list of best practices to encourage fun and fulfilling long-term play.

As the game continues, more and more of the setting can be fleshed out as needed; the players will be conducting their downtime activities outside of sessions, so the GM will be able to know in which direction they will need to add details and properly direct their creative energy. The PCs will be low level and nearly penniless at the beginning of the Campaign - it is trivial to have some NPC point them in the direction of their first dungeon to get the adventure started. If the new GM has a table full of new players, then all the better! The overall structure of the early game is best when it is left simple, the players will be well pleased with even the most standard beginnings, so long as they are consistent. The Campaign, as laid out here, is intended to grow more and more complex at a manageable rate - the GM and the players will develop their understanding of the game together. What starts as spelunking down into a goblin cave can eventually grow into a multi-dimensional adventure with powerful factions and legendary monsters!

The best practices first established by Gary Gygax and Dave Arneson for the creation of a campaign takes into account the needs of the new player and the new GM. The suggestion to keep the initial scope of a campaign bound to a single, small community with a dungeon or two out in the nearby wilderness is not an endorsement of endlessly going on interminable dungeon adventures, it is meant to be an early stage of the GM's gaming career and the lessons learned in a more easily managed environment would provide the GM-Aspirant, as well as players, the room to become more and more fluent in the rules of their mechanical foundation.

Running a game is similar to a physical activity like lifting weights - if someone is brand new to the bench press, is it a wise suggestion for them to put every plate available on the bar? Absolutely not! They should begin with an almost insultingly low weight, so as not to be crushed in their first attempt at lifting. They will slowly grow stronger, adding plates to the bar as they do so - with consistent effort, they will be the ones people look at and marvel.

So it is true of the Campaign: the GM should begin with as simple a scenario as possible, as over time the players will branch out when they feel more and more comfortable doing so; the needs of the game will grow in complexity at a rate that should remain manageable by the GM.

Eventually, as the GM gains mastery over the usage of random tables, full utilization of the freedom afforded by 1:1 time tracking, and general rules fluency of their chosen system the campaign environment will begin to function almost entirely independent of the animating will of the Game Master.

This assertion sounds like the empty, impossible promise to achieve a certain "vibe" or some sort of enlightenment state that is too vague to be true in any meaningful sense.

However it is meant quite literally.

This promised, self-building state of the Campaign is a result of the player characters placing their roots within the setting. It has been alluded to previously, but it needs to be discussed in earnest, specifically; successful player characters who survive will achieve wealth, status, and likely found one or more organizations. It is at this point that the Campaign will fully graduate to Domain Level Play.

The PCs will possess castles, be the heads of guilds, lead companies of mercenaries - they will become movers and shakers within the setting and begin to change it almost entirely independently of the GM's prior knowledge. A PC that manages to become an established noble, for example, will find themselves in a position to enforce their own terms and set their own contracts for lower level player characters, whether it be their own low level alternates, the characters of friends at the table, or even NPCs piloted by the GM.

They achieve a sort of legendary status within the game setting. Particularly ambitious players who reach this rank will engage in all sorts of activities as they push hard to understand what exactly they are made of. Why shouldn't a character like that engage in power struggles with neighbors or sponsor their fellow adventurers to bring them various items and artifacts they may be looking for?

In this way, some adventurers may decide to retire from the field, content to pursue their character goals by hiring others to do the dirty work while launching incredible schemes against their enemies. Such a PC could either be given completely into the hands of the GM, ready-made without any work on their part, or the player could inform the GM out of session what their Domain

Level PCs are working on or otherwise occupied with at any point on the calendar.

Which brings us to the next effort-saving aspect of the Living Campaign: players occasionally want their adventurers to become villains. Often, the contemporary practice in such a case is to require the player who does this to relinquish control of their villainous PC.

This is not necessary through use of the Living Campaign: player activity can be charted outside of the day of the session - a player can still inform the GM what their villainous character is doing and what their goals are, and the GM can arbitrate the results of the activities and personal interactions that the player describes.

There is likely to be a concern with "metagaming" on this point - there is a stigma against combining character knowledge with player knowledge and such practices are decried as a cardinal sin in the gaming community.

Though it can be a problem, it is hardly a campaign-sinking issue that cannot be solved for. The first line of defense for this entire concept is determining the prospective player's ability to cooperate in games such as these before even inviting them to the table; the second line of defense is the lack of concrete information on the part of the player with regard to their villainous PC - often they will simply state what the villain is doing broadly and their goal for doing it in messages to the GM; the last line of defense is the GM themselves. The GM must be ready to ask the question "and how does so-and-so know this information?" when villainous players try to give their evil PC an edge over the party.

As with any time a player pushes the limits of acceptable behavior, it is up to the GM to rein them back in with fair, firm, and friendly authority.

Gradually, the GM will learn to utilize their chosen ruleset with proficiency, where they will have the technical knowledge to create tables and charts of their own for use within their milieu.

Alongside the charts and tables built into the foundational ruleset, the tables the GM develops will help them determine the decisions of various NPCs. It is common for NPCs to be presented with several avenues they might be equally tempted to make, it is in these moments of GM indecision that the outsourcing of final arbitration to a random table will allow the GM the opportunity to be surprised by their creation as well as help prevent common patterns from noticeably developing across multiple NPCs. Sometimes a GM will not be entirely cognizant of their own biases and predilections!

NON-NEGOTIABLE: THE PLAYER STRONGHOLD

Up to this point, the idea of the stronghold is spoken of as a given; the reader may wonder why the player-run holding is considered a non-negotiable necessity for the running of a long term Campaign, especially if they've played in campaigns that did not broach the subject. The stronghold is the permanent home that players' characters have full control over within the game world; the player holding is the mechanism that allows their characters to transcend the need for the dungeon and provides the avenue to higher forms of play better suited for the mid-to-high level game where the stakes grow ever higher and the villains ever more dangerous.

At the start of the Campaign, the PCs were novice adventurers making their way down into the depths for loot and experience - by the time they have a full stronghold of their own, powerful individuals and factions within the setting will begin to mobilize in support of, or against, the player characters. The Lords and Ladies of the Keep are no longer required to venture down below but are better suited for fighting off armies of invaders, tracking down enemies to their urban (or wilderness) hideouts, and/or raising the flag of rebellion against the cruel lord of an impoverished land. These enemies will be renowned warriors, powerful archmages, and high priests with access to all kinds of abilities, connections, and henchmen.

The tense danger of the dungeon in the early levels will fade both because they will become semi-routine and because the PCs will simply have the funds to pursue their initial character motivations which sent them out into the world in the first place.

To challenge the head of a faction, whether legitimate government official or the illegitimate authority of a megalomaniacal magic user, serves the GM and the setting if the players have a point from which their characters can be based and launch their schemes. The Game Master would do themselves and the players a favor if they take the time to consider how and where players might go about procuring property for their characters. It can be anything from a reward for a job well done, to the clearing of a dungeon whose inhabitants were threatening a local community. Encouragement might be warranted if the players express frustration with carrying large sums of money or scaring them a bit with descriptions of the greedy eyes of passersby when the PCs leave thousands of gold coins in rented rooms.

The stronghold also provides an incentive in the possibility of recurring income. The Dungeon primarily serves an economic purpose in the beginning to the middle of a player character's career, but eventually that character's continued travels will involve them with the surface world of nations. They will need some way to keep gold flowing into their coffers, otherwise the progression on their objectives will become halting and intermittent as operations cease and expeditions are then organized to go back into the hostile underground of the Dungeon every time they need more coin.

This is not to say the Dungeon is no longer required: perhaps certain powerful artifacts and items can ONLY be procured through expedition or a well-established character simply wishes to test their strength against a dungeon renowned for its terrible deadliness...it is likely to be the case that the base desire for more gold will cease to be as strong a motivating factor when the player characters are able to organize recurring income through the sale of commodities, collecting of tax revenues, and other industry.

It is also true that stable, permanent lodgings will encourage a stable, permanent Campaign. Being whisked away to combat encounter after combat encounter or from plot point to plot point provides no space for the players to participate in the actual workings of the world...not to mention the player stronghold provides another point of contact through which the setting can affect the players directly: a monster could wander into the hex, enemies could target their home, allies always know where to find them with requests for help or sharing information - there are many possibilities for engagement. After all: in addition to needing something to gain, the players must also have something to lose!

By providing the players with a concrete location that they are responsible for, the GM can spur them to greater heights and naturally transition from a low-level grunt mentality toward the feeling of ownership of immutable aspects of the world. The stronghold is the task the players take on when they have evolved past the need for consistent dungeons and are ready to tackle the considerably deadlier task of challenging organizations, factions, and powerful individuals in the Grand Dungeon known as "Civilization".

NON-NEGOTIABLE: MASSED WARFARE

The typical tabletop RPG table forgoes mass combat in favor of a narrative set piece; this event is often handled no differently than the average dungeon with player investment leaning heavily upon the GM's ability to describe a scene with exciting detail. The castle siege, for example, is a one-off event where the result is usually dependent upon the outcome of several pre-planned "triggers" - perhaps lighting a signal within a certain number of rounds or handling a series of escalating engagements. There are usually no higher tactical decisions at the level of the battle as a whole: there is a clear path forward that is unrelated to things like troop placement, morale, equipment, and overall health of the soldiery.

The common RPG systems will usually release some supplement after a time that includes an entire new subsystem specifically for the gamification of mass combat mechanics and concepts. If any of those subsystems have been adopted as a standard across even a small plurality of tables I am not aware of them. These add-ons are nearly always very different from the mechanics that they are supposed to be attached to; the general play of these games do nothing to prepare the player for the unique system suddenly foisted upon them and as a result they gain notoriety for being a useless, boring extra bit of rules by the greater playerbase.

This is usually noted without fanfare, as a matter of course, and it is not uncommon for the very notion of viable mass combat to be derided as an impossible goal that requires compromises be made by turning the whole endeavor into a mere "scene".

Not only is it possible, but accommodations for mass combat are *necessary* for the progression of the Campaign! The greater villains of high level play are almost always the heads of organizations of their own with fighting men moving into many theaters of battle to cause all kinds of havoc; even powerful player characters will need the support of dedicated fighters so as not to be overwhelmed or held in place while the villains flit about, accomplishing their objectives. The idea that such things are not able to be fulfilled with the tools provided within the foundational ruleset is an assumption that has stymied the potential of many, many tables. If a GM's players have enjoyed combat encounters at the skirmish level then why is it not true that they can't enjoy it at the army level?

A functioning mass combat system is capable of creating emergent situations and events within a scenario that will be far more organic and immersive to the discerning table; the collapse of a defensive line, the dramatic push for control of a gatehouse, the unforeseen forest ambush...these situations, well executed, will be burned into the minds of the players and delight them as they retell the stories to friends. They will recall that time when they and their compatriots had to take cover from arrow fire en route to relieve a besieged town or when their mercenaries fled the field after unexpectedly heavy casualties, forcing the PCs to make a desperate last stand with the remaining soldiers until more successful allies could redirect to relieve them.

It might be said that large-scale combat is so complicated as to slow the game session down to an unforgivable degree. Such a position speaks to a certain defeatist attitude that must be striven against whenever possible (both in life and the game!): a serious effort to make potential scenarios playable and fun ought to be undertaken before being declared non-feasible.

The progenitor d20 systems and rules from which large portions of the hobby is derived is robust enough to function quite well at a 10x or even a 20x scale (see APPROACHING MASS COMBAT; pg. 64). This alters very little about the underlying combat system that players should already be familiar with at this point in the game. A short explanation and perhaps a low-stakes, small encounter will be all that's needed to help players apply knowledge that they already possess at a grander scale.

Functionally, the development of unrelated, tangential mass combat systems that run parallel to the foundational ruleset serve as poorer, low-resolution game-within-a-game. To implement them is to expect the players to embrace a new, worse, game that they did not agree to - but was smuggled onto their table through the initial rulebooks that they HAD agreed upon. While scaling up skirmish combat is mechanically consistent with what the players already know, the primary reason to scale up existing rules rather than developing said parallel system is that everyone around the table is not suddenly saddled with unnecessary work with a half-baked product.

It's easier to tell them: "do what you have been doing, but 10x the numbers." - this way is more respectful of their time and easier for the GM to referee as the rules will support the basic structure of the combat, as the scale of the numbers is the only thing to have substantially changed.

The insistence on preparing for this type of play is based on the assumption that a high level player character is likely to grow into a powerful figure in their region (otherwise known as a "Patron); the inclusion of these aspects are obvious as certain PCs are required to think at the regional scale and thus will have need of soldiers that they can move about here and there to be realistically in control of their fiefs. It is the logical progression, then, that a PC fighting force would need to have some sort of governing mechanical base that informs the player as to their use; otherwise they are transparently mere narrative tools meant to manipulate the perception of the players if the GM never intended them to have any meaningful control over the assets at their disposal.

This in-built dismissal of the players' control plays a significant role in the widespread problems with player involvement and immersion. Tightly controlled scenarios only allow for emergent phenomena insofar as the GM allows it to be so or fails to perceive a particularly creative approach by one or more players. Placing the power of such decisions firmly in the hands of players, giving them full access to the flow of information via direct troop movement on the battlefield (rather than a description of soldiers fighting or some pre-ordained cavalry charge), and then allowing them to react to their victory or their defeat on their own direct orders promises to engage them ever further with the Campaign.

A lost battle could serve as the origin story for a henchman or a new player character; a tremendous victory could draw a new ally's attention, further growing a Patron's influence and authority within the Campaign.

A campaign that achieves this level of play will see that Patrons who are particularly active or creative within the setting makes the job of the GM much easier - they are almost GMs themselves at this point with the way they drive the game!

THE PERPETUAL MOTION MACHINE

In the end, there is nothing else like the Tabletop RPG. This truth is ultimately what keeps a campaign running during its duration...and its duration can run long. If the Game Master so desires it, a campaign can continue indefinitely without ever losing the requisite number of players to continue playing. Individuals may drop in and out due to unavoidable real-world obligations, but a successful campaign will always have potential replacement members waiting in the wings.

Refer to the many articles and stories discussing the crushing lack of Game Masters to run games relative to the enormous number of players who wish to play in them: how much more a desirable commodity is the GM who runs their game with proficiency and ever growing expertise?

The Campaign is not required to enter into a final act as though it is a television series or traditional video game. Perhaps the stories of individual player characters will conclude in a way similar to the end of a movie or a particularly long-lived storyline that is resolved will provide that feeling of satisfaction from an awaited conclusion, but the Campaign *overall* need not end or even go on hiatus!

"Stories" exist in the real world; the "main character" is the person experiencing their life. The players will feel something similar to that, where their PC is the hero of their own "story" in a world that is refereed by the GM...but the responsibility for *enacting* this "story" is reversed and thrown back onto that player; the Game Master does not hand down a definitive narrative that tells players what to think and how to feel, by this method.

It seems entirely possible that concluding a typical story-driven campaign runs the risk of losing players unduly between the end of a GM's Campaign 1 and the beginning of their Campaign 2, which is certainly a waste!

Now the reasons for conducting a game this way is understandable: the grueling effort of running a story-driven campaign, directed like a movie/written like a book, will eventually require the Game Master to take a break to rest and recover before sallying forth once again to start it all over and/or the players will reach the highest level possible with an individual character and would like to play someone new of a different class.

A Living Campaign is not subject to this limiting criteria and the players can play many characters as far as they would like and retire individuals when they have had their fill of them or it feels appropriate to do so. The players, being far more involved and driving large storylines via their actions and requests, share the load of narrative progression and planning with their GM and alleviating significant portions of the stress of refereeing a campaign. The only reason then that a Game Master would need to stop conducting their campaign is because they simply feel like stopping - a perfectly good reason that is entirely unrelated to the availability of individual players or the taking on of a too-heavy workload with regard to session planning.

If anything, the loss of a player or two will have the opposite problem: the GM will find that they have more applicants than seats available! Refer to IN PREPARATION FOR THE CAMPAIGN (see pg.13), where the recommendation for a filter was suggested. Any such filter should be tailored to the needs and circumstances of the Game Master employing them: the filter for a first-time GM only needs to select an initial crop of players that is likely to get along and will be patient as the GM learns to play the game and add on to their milieu over time, the long-time Game Master's filter might need to be a bit more (or less) discerning and sophisticated (depending on their goals for the game).

The "Veteran" GM might be known as such within their community and a particularly long-running campaign will have the attention of interested parties that would like to join at earliest opportunity. It is possible that the needs of their initial filter will have some criteria for cycling out individual players: perhaps when all of a player's related player characters are deceased or other some-such tragedy, for example, so as to better serve the community...if it is their wish to do so.

By all means, play as exclusively as desired!

Why shouldn't the world of the Campaign continue for years or decades? The Game Master who continually pushes themselves to higher heights of efficiency and creativity is not destined to burn out in one-to-two years time. With each passing year, they may find new things to love about the Campaign they have created and continually excite their passion so that it never fully fades. Perfectly successful adults find joy in creative hobbies like assembling model planes or creating elaborate systems of model trains; hobbies that evolve with the maturing of the individual who takes them on.

So it is with Tabletop RPGs: a GM's skill and desire with regard to running a campaign can mature in the same way as any other hobby - it can be grown to accommodate the more sophisticated adult mind as the best practices of the teenage years begin to fail due to the accrual of responsibilities and the narrowing of available free time.

Simply put: the hobbyist must get better at the hobby if they want to keep it.

TO THE PROLIFERATION OF TABLES

The purpose of this work is to aid in the creation of more stable, long-term campaigns so that many others will be able to partake in this hobby for years to come. It is understood that perhaps there are a number of ways for a group of friends to create a style of game that will see them playing together indefinitely, it is also true that not all of these styles are created equal to one another, at least in terms of their ability to iterate.

It is my hope that the advice contained within these pages will aid in the broader discussion and help create a new, alternate standard through which a larger percentage of new campaigns will survive the initial stages of creation than they do at present.

Far from being overly restrictive, the commands of each chapter provide a strong framework that a dazzling domain can be built upon. There is a general reluctance in many corners to speak with significant authority in these matters, the only conviction seems to be "do what thou whilst" with all forms of advice qualified with many asterisks of disclosure.

In the interest of clarity and respecting the reader, the information contained here was written in such a way as to bluntly explain my beliefs as the author of this book. It is my hope that the words contained will at least convey a certain conviction that the reader will at least consider.

I strongly hold that a Living Campaign CAN be replicated across many tables and rules systems, and that many of those Game Masters can be saved from the disintegration of their games and the wasting of all of their work thus far. Through diligent implementation of the above described practices, Game Master and

Player can achieve a synthesis and mutual responsibility for the continuation and evolution of a campaign conducted over a very long period of time without cessation. Hopefully, such campaigns will beget more campaigns as the participating players cultivate the skills needed to one day run a table of their own and create a network of intertwined, participating games that players will be able to freely go between.

For those that yet have doubts and have nonetheless read this work in its entirety: what would be the issue with simply attempting what I have described here? If such a reader is currently conducting a game in the contemporary manner and does not wish to jar the players with significant changes to the running of their game, that is certainly understandable - eventually though such a campaign will reach its natural conclusion, as all stories do, and then why not ground it in the framework of the *Living Campaign* in the lead up to "Campaign 2"?

A personal setting, 1:1 time, formalized dungeon exploration, player driven adventures, encumbrance, experience and leveling criteria, and the preparation for mass combat are the lynchpin pieces that can make a campaign extremely durable and sustain both the Game Master's enthusiasm for creation and the Players' continuing, reliable participation in the game.

It is my hope that *The Living Campaign* has prepared prospective GMs for the creation and running of their own sturdy, stable games and that they successfully carry the hobby forward into the future!

Made in the USA
Las Vegas, NV
24 June 2025

24039114R00085